"It's time for her therapy," Ms. Tortunesky announced. She pointed to me as she said "her." This was because she refuses to call me Star, which she insists is not the name God and my parents gave me. However, the one time she called me Stella I managed to by-mistake-on-purpose cough up all my phlegm on her. I grant you it was disgusting, but it did the trick.

Oh, no, another session of her horrible thumps. The very thought of it made my stomach queasy and I broke out in a sweat. It felt like everyone in the room was staring at me, feeling sorry for me, just like they felt sorry for Sally. I hated that more than anything in the world.

CHERIE BENNETT is the author of many books for young adults. She lives with her husband in Nashville, Tennessee.

Day by Day

Good-bye, Best Friend
Cherie Bennett

LAUREL-LEAF BOOKS

Published by
Dell Publishing
a division of
Bantam Doubleday Dell Publishing Group, Inc.
666 Fifth Avenue
New York, New York 10103

The trademark Laurel-Leaf Library® is registered in the U.S. Patent and Trademark Office.

The trademark Dell® is registered in the U.S. Patent and Trademark Office.

ISBN: 0-440-21247-2

RL: 5.2

Printed in the United States of America

June 1992

10 9 8 7 6 5 4 3 2 1

OPM

The author wishes to thank Dr. Peter Gottesfeld of Peekskill, New York, for the medical information, and Jacquie Gordon for writing the moving story of her daughter Christine's struggle with cystic fibrosis, *Give Me One Wish*. It was invaluable in my research.

For Judy "Girl-chick" Harris,
my best friend

PROLOGUE

Contrary to what it says on my birth certificate, my name is not Stella Johnella Grubner. My name is Star—no last name, thank you very much. I renamed myself when I was six years old, which was seven years ago. That's when I saw my first Madonna video. If she only needed one name, I only needed one name. You might call that precocious thinking for a six-year-old. I call it survival.

Adults should keep the consequences in mind when they name their children. Take my parents, for example. They were already stuck with the last name Grubner, which, let's face it, is excruciating. So do they turn to each other and say, "Let's give the kid a break and give her a really cool first name"? They do not.

When my parents got married my dad was a stand-up comic and my mom was an actress and a dancer, and they lived in New York City. When my mom found out she was pregnant with me, she had just started rehearsals for a revival of this famous play, *A Streetcar Named Desire*. She had to drop out of the play because of me (which leads me to believe I was your basic unplanned-for event), so she named me Stella after the character she never got to play.

As for my middle name, there is this movie she loved called *Saturday Night Fever*, in which John Travolta is supposed to be this fabulous dancer from a poor background (sort of like my mother, I guess). That's how she came up with Johnella. But I ask you, are those any reasons to burden an innocent child with such hideous names?

I figure the reason that my father let my mother name me whatever she wanted is that he felt really bad about my mother having to give up being in the play. That part I'm not sure about, since I've never actually met my father. He left when I was an infant. I don't think he ever got famous, because I haven't seen him on *The Tonight Show*. Claudia—that's my mom— says she thinks he's in Los Angeles. I try to watch the comedy cable network, because a lot of those shows are from Los Angeles. He might show up there. Even if he was smart enough to change his name from Gary Grubner, I just know I'd recognize him the instant I saw him.

Anyway, after I was born and my dad left, Claudia ran out of money, so she moved back home to where her parents lived. That's how we ended up here in Somerset, Indiana, and that's why even though I was born in New York City, I don't remember living there at all. Now my mom teaches acting and dancing to kids, and she has the lead in all the Somerset Community Theater productions. Her parents ended up retiring and moving to Florida, and they gave my mom their house. Somerset is okay, if you like boring little midwestern towns. Personally, I plan to take off for New York as soon as I get out of high school. I'm going to be a very famous actress one day. I figure since I study with tutors and don't actually go to school, I can get four years of high school done in three, and be in New York before I even hit my seventeenth birthday.

This is a good plan, since there is a good chance I won't live to see my twentieth birthday.

Not that I buy that. Not for an instant. The thing is, I have this disease called cystic fibrosis. My doctors and my mother never really talk to me about it. Of course, I don't ask them either. I think their attitude is "Ask me no questions, I'll tell you no lies." I could always tell that they really, really did not want me to ask.

So one day when I was ten I went to the library and looked it up. I can tell you just what the medical dictionary said, because I have it memorized. It said: "Cystic fibrosis is an inherited disease of the exocrine glands. Abnormal mucus produced in the lungs breeds chronic lung infections. The infections cause erosion of the surrounding tissue, which results in bleeding from the lungs. This disease was discovered in 1938. In 1961 the average life expectancy was five years. Today the average life expectancy is nineteen years. To date this disease is always fatal."

Fatal. As in dead. I admit that one threw me for a minute. Then I read it again. "The average life expectancy is nineteen years." I checked the date of the book. It was written in 1981. Maybe things had improved since then. I mean, things had certainly improved since 1961. Besides, they were talking about "averages." Well, I am not average. I am extraordinary.

So when I was ten years old, sitting there in the library with this medical dictionary in front of me, I decided that I am not going to die. I'm just not.

Despite the fact that I don't usually look or

even feel very sick, I have to admit this stupid disease is very inconvenient. Like, for example, the part about my having tutors. I've never actually gone to a regular school. Well, I started in kindergarten, but I coughed so much that the teacher said I was upsetting the other kids. My mother got mad. My disease is not catching or anything—either you're born with it, or you aren't. Some people don't understand about illness at all. They just get scared. And they don't want you to cough on them.

I've had the same tutor since I was six years old. Her name is Liza-Jayne and she's from Tennessee. She has a southern accent that I can mimic perfectly. Liza-Jayne is around thirty, I think, and she thinks she's very plain, which she is not. She has shaggy brown hair and big brown eyes. She is sort of bony looking, but she has very large breasts, which I think makes her embarrassed, so she wears baggy sweaters all the time. If I were fortunate enough to grow very large breasts I would wear things like red sequined bras and see-through shirts with nothing underneath. Of course Claudia—my mother likes me to call her Claudia—is flat as a board, and so far I am too, so I doubt that I will get to live out that particular fantasy.

When I'm home Liza-Jayne teaches me there

and when I'm in Hope House, she teaches me here. That's where I'm writing this—Hope House. My home away from home. Ugh.

Hope House is a place for sick kids. I've probably slept here more nights than I've slept in my own bed. Every time I get sick, I get readmitted. The good news is it doesn't look like a hospital. It's not nearly as bad as St. Stephen's Hospital, where I've had to go when I've been really sick. The bad news is that if I'm at Hope House, it means my health has taken a turn for the worse.

That's what my doctor, Dr. Pembroke, always says when I have to be readmitted to Hope House. "Well, Star (at least he's bright enough to call me Star), your lungs seem to have taken a turn for the worse." He always rubs his beard when he says this. I think he finds it comforting. After that he tells Claudia I have to go back into Hope House, and I get admitted the same day.

What happened a few weeks ago just seemed like the usual routine. After Dr. Pembroke listened to my lungs, Claudia and I sat in his office. As soon as he started stroking that beard I knew where I was going. I figured my stay at Hope House would be the same as always. But it wasn't the same. Everything changed. And that's what I'm going to write about. If I live long enough to get really famous, maybe I can tell it myself on *Arsenio*. But just in case I don't, I'm writing it all down. This is the truth, or my name isn't Star.

I

1

"Star! Looking good!"

"Hey, Star, welcome home!"

"Whoa, Star, great jacket! Can I borrow it?"

I waved to my friends as I bopped down to the corner room on the second floor of Hope House.

"Ah, Hope House, how do I love thee? Let me count the ways," I muttered sarcastically as I dumped my oversized carpetbag on the bed.

Sally Kasem stuck her head in the door. We're the same age, and we've known each other for years. She gets admitted pretty often for her brittle diabetes. We've even been roommates a couple of times. Sally is not, as my mother would say, a rocket scientist. Sometimes her dumbness really gets to me. Other times I think it's something she cultivates to get attention. She does have really nice green eyes, wavy blond hair, and an overbite. When I was little I thought her overbite was the coolest thing ever, and I walked around with my upper lip stuck out, pretending I had one too. Sally pinched me hard in the recreation room one day during finger painting. Claudia said Sally was mad because she thought I was making fun of her.

"I don't know how you do it, Star, but you always do it," Sally said as she sat down on the other bed. "I begged to get the corner room this time, but it was no deal. I'm stuck in 1-A with some kid who talks out loud to her Barbie dolls. And here you waltz in and get the corner room again, and you don't even have a room-mate!"

I plopped down on the bed, using my carpet-bag as a pillow. "This room should have my name on the door. And a star," I added with a serene smile.

It is a great room. It's almost twice as big as the seven other bedrooms, and it has huge corner windows that look out over the back porch and the gardens. There's even a window seat, covered with forest-green and white print cushions.

Sally sighed, looking around the room. "Maybe I could transfer in here," she said hopefully.

"Nope. I'm getting a roommate, Ms. McG. just told me downstairs," I said. "Her name is Courtney something-or-other. She's never been here before."

"Well, I don't see why some new girl should get the best room," Sally sniffed. Sally is one of those people who always feel left out, or mistreated, or both.

"How come you're here again, anyway?" I asked Sally, pulling off my black cowboy boots. I had been in Hope House three months previously, and Sally had been in too. Usually she only showed up once for about every four or five of my admissions.

"Oh, they need to regulate my insulin again or something," Sally said with a sigh. She stared covetously at my cowboy boots. She had told me before that her parents refused to let her buy any. "How come you're back?"

"Same old same old." I grunted, finally prying my boots off. I brushed my copper-colored curls out of my face impatiently and settled back down on my carpetbag. Talking about my illness is one of my least favorite things in the world to do, so I changed the subject. "So, how's the local talent?"

Sally shrugged. "One cute guy in 2-B, but he just came in yesterday and I haven't talked to him yet. I don't know what he's in for. Other than that, there's just Dr. Steve."

"Never say 'just' before you say 'Dr. Steve,' " I instructed. "Dr. Steve is a serious hunk."

As if on cue, Dr. Steve came bounding into my room. Dr. Steven Rhodes is a heart surgeon. He's about thirty years old and he is gorgeous. He has coffee-colored skin, deep-set dark eyes, and Claudia says he has the "body of death." Fortunately Claudia is too old for him, whereas I am mature for my age.

"I heard from Ms. McGehan that you were here," Dr. Steve said. "I thought I'd pop in and say hello. How are you doing?"

I gave him my most brilliant smile, not unlike Paula Abdul's in her diet Coke commercial. "Oh, fine," I said breezily.

Dr. Steve gave me a look that said he knew better—if I were fine, I wouldn't be back at Hope House.

"Okay, I coughed up some blood last night," I admitted. "Not much, though."

"You're going on IV antibiotics, I take it," Dr. Steve said.

"Yeah," I said with a sigh, indicating, I hoped, that it was a trivial matter. "I feel great, though. Don't I look great?" I batted my eyelashes at him the way Scarlett O'Hara does in *Gone With the Wind.*

Dr. Steve laughed. "That is called fishing for compliments, Star," he said, wagging his finger at me.

"And?" I prompted him.

"And yes, you look great," he admitted with a smile. "Your hair got longer."

"That's because I haven't been here for three entire months. That's a record for me," I told him. "Not that I didn't miss you and pine away for you and everything," I added seriously.

Sally giggled and put her hand over her mouth. Sally is so juvenile.

Dr. Steve shook his head. "You are going to be hazardous to some guy's health when you start dating."

"Not some guy, lots of guys . . . I hope!" I said fervently. "Hey, you want to come back later and play some poker? I brought my lucky deck!"

Dr. Steve laughed. "Last time we played for pennies you took five dollars off me. I think your lucky deck is only lucky for you."

"Well, of course," I said indignantly, "that's the whole point!"

Even Sally was bright enough to get why that was funny, and all three of us started laughing. Before I could stop myself my laugh turned into a cough. The cough was dry and metallic-sounding, and I had trouble catching my breath.

Dr. Steve patted my back in a circular, comforting motion as the cough finally peaked and slowed. It was almost nice enough to make the coughing attack worth it.

"How many thumps are you doing each day?" he asked, a frown on his face.

"Oh, please," I barely managed, since I hadn't really caught my breath yet. "Don't talk to me about thumps. At home I've been doing two, but The Torturer says I have to start doing three a day. It's her idea of a good time."

Both Dr. Steve and Sally knew who The Torturer was. Ms. Tortunesky looks like The Incredible Hulk, only she's not green and she wears a dress. She used to be an army nurse, but she retired. Personally, I think she did this just so she could make my life miserable. It is her job to do the daily physical therapy on me and any other kids with cystic fibrosis who happen to be in Hope House.

She lives only two blocks away. Every morning she wakes me up at six A.M. by barking commands in my face. Then we do the therapy. We repeat the whole thing at night. And the last time I'd seen her The Torturer said I needed to add an afternoon session too.

I hate thumps more than just about anything

in the world. See, the problem with cystic fibrosis is that my body produces too much of a bad kind of phlegm. The thumps help clear this gross, thick phlegm out of my lungs. If I don't get rid of this stuff, I get pneumonia. They can treat pneumonia with antibiotics, but there are only so many different kinds of antibiotics, and after one kind is used over and over, it stops working—the bugs just becomes resistant to it. So then they have to find another one, but eventually the same thing happens. If it gets really, really bad, my lungs bleed. That's dangerous. And scary. I should know, because it's happened to me a few times. The thumps are supposed to keep my lungs clear—it's preventative medicine. So I guess I should be grown up about it, since thumps are supposed to be saving my life and everything. I still hate them.

You see, I have to lie tilted downward on a stack of pillows while The Torturer pounds on different parts of my chest, shoulders, sides, and back. We're not talking gentle pats here, we're talking serious smacks, fast, one right after the other. It always feels like she's beating me up. Before the thumps I have to inhale this horrible stuff called Mucomyst through an oxygen mask. After the thumps I have to sit up and make myself cough, over and over, as hard as I can. This is supposed to dislodge some of the mucus. Then I have to breathe the Mucomyst stuff again. The whole process is exhausting and it takes forever. At home Claudia does the thumps. She doesn't hit half as hard as Ms. Tortunesky.

"She's actually not a bad person," Dr. Steve said. "She's just kind of . . . serious."

"Serious?" I snorted. "She's sadistic! She gets thrills from her work!" I jumped up and folded my arms, furrowed my brow, and sucked in my cheeks. Instantly I turned into a tiny version of The Torturer. "Turn over! Lie still! This ought to help! Now cough!" I barked in my perfect imitation of Ms. Tortunesky. I whacked my hand through the air after each command, just the way she pounded mercilessly on my back.

"Wow, that's great," Sally said, giggling. "You sound just like her!"

"I admit you have talent," Dr. Steve said, trying not to smile. "But you have to realize, she's trying to help you."

"Go back to the part about how I have talent," I suggested, sitting back down on the bed.

"You do, I've told you before," Dr. Steve said.

"Gee, thanks," I said.

So as not to waste my talent completely, I have been known to act out a scene or two at

Hope House, putting on shows for the staff and the other kids. I am forced to write these scenes myself, as there are so few truly great roles for a thirteen-year-old.

"Maybe you'll become an actress," Dr. Steve said.

"Maybe?" I repeated. I was cut to the quick. I already considered myself an actress. On the other hand, doing scenes for the staff at Hope House in Somerset, Indiana, can't exactly be looked at as the big time.

"Do you realize how young Drew Barrymore was when she started her career?" I asked Dr. Steve, falling back on my bed.

He shrugged his shoulders.

"There are thirteen-year-olds starring in their own television series, and in really big movies," I told him. "I'm getting too old to be discovered young!"

"Everything's so dramatic with her," Sally said to Dr. Steve, rolling her eyes.

I glared at Sally. I was very glad she'd gotten a tiny room and a roommate who played with Barbie dolls.

"Star, you sweetheart, you!" Andrea Shepherd sang out as she ran into my room. Andrea and her husband, Ben, are both social workers, and they live at Hope House. It's hard to believe that they're married to each other. First of all, Andrea is about four inches taller than Ben, and she must outweigh him by at least thirty pounds. Second of all, their personalities are totally opposite. Andrea is very enthusiastic and funny and energetic, always cracking jokes, and running around hugging people. I've never heard her say a mean word about anybody. Ben is very quiet, and kind of shy. He listens carefully but he hardly ever talks. He never, ever cracks a joke, although he does laugh at Andrea's, and he never, ever hugs anyone. Well, I suppose he hugs Andrea in private —at least I hope he does.

When Andrea finished hugging me, I noticed that something was missing—about ten inches of her perfect jet-black hair.

"You cut it!" I said, pointing in horror.

"Hey, it's not a major felony!" Andrea said with a laugh.

"You have the most perfect hair in the world, and you cut it!" I said.

Andrea felt her short-cropped black tresses. "Is this your way of telling me you don't like it?" she asked me.

"Does Ben like it?" I asked her slyly.

"He said it's interesting, which probably means he hates it," Andrea admitted. "Oh, so what? I like it, and it'll grow back."

I folded my arms under my head and sighed.

"Well, it's a tragedy of monumental importance, if you ask me."

Suddenly I felt warm—sometimes I do after a coughing fit—so I sat up to take off my rhinestone-studded denim jacket. Then a thought occurred to me. "Hey, what day is it?"

"Thursday," Sally piped up. This level of information was right up Sally's alley.

"Thursday!" I moaned. "Oh, no, tell me it isn't Thursday!"

"Yes," Andrea said darkly, "it's the day of the dreaded *M* food."

"Meat loaf!" we all cried at once.

Every Thursday the cook, Ms. Brady, makes her famous meat loaf. It's famous for all the wrong reasons. My theory is that she takes the leftovers from the entire week, combines them with mystery meat, smothers the whole thing in tomato sauce so nothing can actually be identified, and calls it meat loaf. Since no one ever eats the meat loaf, I have another theory. All the leftover meat loafs are frozen, and then they're added to yet another meat loaf. It's like some kind of science-fiction food that just keeps mutating.

"Quick, Sally, hand me the phone."

Sally pushed the phone, which stood on the nightstand between the two beds, my way. She knew exactly who I was calling. So did Andrea and Dr. Steve. They all waited, trying not to actually lick their lips.

"Rats, busy signal," I said, hanging up the phone.

All three faces sagged. They knew I was calling my aunt Amy, of Amy's Edibles Gourmet Shoppe. Her food is famous throughout Somerset, throughout Indiana, even. She invented a dessert called Tall, Dark, and Chocolate that won first prize in the International Gourmet Foods Dessert Contest. Aunt Amy traveled all over, appearing on talk shows with famous people, showing them how to make her dessert. Whenever I get admitted to Hope House, I always perk up my diet with a steady stream of goodies from Aunt Amy's. Fortunately for me I don't have any dietary restrictions like so many of the other kids. And being the kind of girl I am, I often share with my hungry friends.

"Only your aunt can save me from the *M* food," Sally said, grabbing my wrist. "My parents are coming by for dinner tonight. They think the *M* food is nutritious. They'll hover over me and make me eat every morsel. You've got to help me!"

And Sally said *I* was dramatic. "Try to control yourself," I told her coolly. I pulled a pen and some scrap paper from my carpetbag.

"I'll keep trying Aunt Amy's phone number

until I get through," I assured everyone. "Okeydokey, get your orders in," I said, my pen poised over the paper.

"Fried chicken bits!" Sally screamed. "Mmmmmm, they're awesome! Oh, and some double-chocolate Oreo-cookie ice cream," she added.

"Tall, Dark, and Chocolate is my weakness in life," Andrea confessed.

"That'll be two orders for you." I nodded, writing it down. I looked at Dr. Steve.

"How about that homemade pizza?" he asked.

"But no anchovies!" Sally and Andrea screamed at the same time.

"Uck," I said. "No offense, Dr. Steve, but how can you ruin perfectly good pizza with those dead, slimy, bony little fish?"

"I love anchovies!" Dr. Steve protested.

"No anchovies!" we all screamed at him. Somehow that started everyone laughing, which started me coughing again, which caused Dr. Steve to start thumping me hard on the back, and Andrea and Sally to start yelling suggestions and offering help, all at the same time.

The door opened, and into this melee walked my new roommate, Courtney Cambridge. And Courtney Cambridge looked scared to death.

2

Courtney Cambridge was one of those perfect-looking girls that you see in magazine ads. I assessed her quickly. Prettier than me. Taller than me. Healthier looking than me. Breasts. It was hate at first sight.

"Oh, sorry," Courtney mumbled from the doorway. She looked ready to fall over from fright.

"Courtney!" Dr. Steve cried, his face lighting up with happiness.

Oh, great. She already knew Dr. Steve.

"Am I in the right room?" she asked tentatively.

"This is the right room," Dr. Steve assured her. "This is Courtney Cambridge," he told us. "She's a patient of mine."

Correction. She didn't just know him. She

was a patient of his. Things were going down-hill fast.

"Maybe I should have waited for my parents . . ." Courtney faltered.

"No, no, it's fine," Dr. Steve told her. He walked over to her, put his arm around her shoulders, and led her gently into the room.

Dr. Steve introduced Sally and Andrea. "And this is Star, your roommate," Dr. Steve finished.

"Your name is Star?" Courtney asked, wide-eyed.

"Uh-huh," I said, acting terribly bored. Dr. Steve still had his arm around her shoulders. I wanted to snatch her perfect blond hair out of her head.

Dr. Steve led her to the other bed, forcing an unhappy Sally to relinquish her position on it. Sally sighed as she stood up, thinking, I'm sure, that the bed should have been hers.

Courtney perched on the very edge of the bed, as if she were about to bolt from the room at any second.

"You and Star will get along great, I'm sure," Dr. Steve said with an encouraging smile at his little darling. "Are your parents downstairs?"

Courtney nodded. "Filling out forms," she answered.

"That'll take forever," I said knowingly.

"Why don't you lie down, Courtney," Dr. Steve suggested gently.

"No, no, I'm fine," she said quickly. She was clutching her purse in her lap so hard that her knuckles were turning white.

"Well, I have to run," Andrea said, getting up from her chair. "It was nice meeting you, Courtney. Just let me know if I can help you in any way," she added with a friendly smile.

"Hey, stop by later for your chocolate fix!" I called to Andrea as she walked out the door.

"You just relax, Courtney," Dr. Steve told her. "You'll be having another EKG soon, and I'll be back to talk to you later."

"Don't forget our date!" I reminded him. "I'll bring the pizza, you bring the beer."

Dr. Steve laughed and winked at me. "It's a date," he said, waving as he walked out the door.

"They let you have beer?" Courtney asked in a shocked voice.

"Sure," I said. "And on Sunday we have champagne."

Sally, who had been standing between our beds all this time staring at Courtney, cracked up.

"You're joking," Courtney figured out.

"There you are!" came a lilting voice from

the door. It belonged to Ms. McGehan, who we all call Ms. McG. She's in her fifties, but she seems even older to me because she's sort of old-fashioned looking. She has very, very long white hair that she wears up in a variety of beautiful combs. She also has this great singing voice, with a kind of lilt to it since she's from Ireland. She told me once that she moved away from Ireland over thirty years ago, but she still has that certain sound to her voice. It's very comforting, to tell you the truth.

Ms. McG. pointed a finger at Sally. "You. Blood time, dear heart." She noticed Courtney sitting like a statue on the edge of the bed, and smiled at her. "Oh, hello, dear. I see you found your room."

"Yes," Courtney whispered.

"Good. This is the nicest room we have," Ms. McG. added kindly. She turned her attention to Sally, who looked extremely peeved that the room wasn't hers. "Well, come on, then," Ms. McG. said briskly. "Let's get cracking."

"Oh, I feel like a pincushion," Sally complained.

"Not to worry, dear heart, I'm taking it myself, and you know I'm the best blood-taker there is," Ms. McG. assured Sally.

"Not a really terrific thing to be known for, Ms. McG.," I observed.

"I'll be back for some of yours later," Ms. McG. promised me as she shepherded Sally from the room.

"Don't forget my chicken and ice cream!" Sally yelled on her way out the door.

"You got it," I yelled back. Not that I was so anxious to do a favor for Sally, but it couldn't hurt for Courtney to see how important I was. I picked up the phone and dialed Aunt Amy's again.

"I hope you're hungry," I said to Courtney as the phone rang.

"Not really," she murmured.

My aunt finally answered the phone.

"Hi, it's me!" I cried. "Listen, I'm a desperate girl. It's meat loaf night at the prison. . . ."

Aunt Amy knew just what I meant. She's very nice about supplying me with food during my various jail terms.

"Let's see, a couple of orders of fried chicken bits, one pizza with everything but anchovies, a couple dozen oatmeal-raisin cookies, some Oreo-cookie ice cream, and . . . hold on a second, Aunt Amy." I took my mouth from the phone and looked at Courtney. "You like chocolate?" I asked her.

"Sure," said Courtney, completely bewildered.

I went back to the phone. "And six orders of Tall, Dark, and Chocolate," I said.

"You must really be hungry," my aunt joked. She knew I shared with everyone at Hope House.

"Ravenous," I agreed with a laugh.

"I'll be done here about six, and then I'll stop by with the smuggled goods," she told me.

"Can't wait," I said, hanging up. Courtney was just staring at me. I explained about my aunt owning Amy's Edibles.

"I've seen that store," Courtney said. "Are we allowed to bring in our own food?"

"We are if no one catches us," I told her smugly.

"Oh," she said.

What a girl. What a conversationalist. Obviously she thought she could get by on her looks. She didn't seem to care that I'd just ordered her about ten dollars' worth of to-die-for chocolate desserts. But then again, she still seemed scared to death, so maybe dessert wasn't high on her list of priorities.

"You might as well get comfortable," I told her. "You're probably going to be here awhile." Watching her poised there on the edge of her bed was starting to make me nervous.

Courtney sat back a little, her hands still

firmly clenched around her little black purse. She didn't say anything.

"So, how old are you?" I finally asked her, just to break the silence.

"Thirteen," she said.

"Same as me," I told her.

Silence.

Okay. I'd try again.

"So, what are you here for?" I asked. Before she could answer me, I started to cough. I tried to will it back—usually I can—but this one got the best of me. Oh, great. Now this new girl was going to hear me make my disgusting hacking noises.

"Do you have a bad cold or something?" Courtney asked when I finally stopped coughing.

"Cystic fibrosis," I told her when I could talk again. "It's, like, this lung thing." I shrugged it off as if it were nothing. "So what about you?"

Courtney pressed her lips together until they turned white, and took a ragged breath. "I'm not sure. I just had this bad sore throat. I didn't tell my mom right away because I didn't want to miss this big away game we had. So then it got worse and worse. It turned out to be strep throat. And then somehow from that I got rheumatic fever. And now they think it did something to my heart." Her hands were shaking as much as her voice. Frankly, the girl was a nervous wreck. I had to say something to calm her down.

"Can't be that bad," I told her. "Your lips aren't blue and your nails aren't blue. If something is mega-wrong with your heart, you turn blue."

"Are you sure?" Courtney asked hopefully.

"Sure I'm sure," I told her. "I don't think you have too much to worry about."

She smiled for the first time. Wouldn't you know she had dimples. "Thanks for telling me," she said. "No one will tell me anything."

"Yeah, well, that's how doctors are," I said philosophically.

"I've never been sick before," she confided. "Well, I had the measles when I was a kid, but you know what I mean."

I nodded. I myself had never not been sick, but who was I to quibble?

"You don't seem very sick either," she told me, "except for your cough."

I shrugged. "No big thing."

"Yeah, I guess not," Courtney said, clearly relieved. She settled back on the bed, finally relinquishing her stranglehold on her purse. "You know, I was so nervous coming up here," she admitted. "Walking down the hall, I saw

some really sick-looking kids. Two of them
were bald!"

"Chemo," I said knowingly.

"That means they have cancer and they're
getting chemotherapy, right?" Courtney asked.
She shuddered. "It was so horrible. I just
prayed I wouldn't have a really sick roommate."

Well, silent Courtney now seemed to be on a
roll. So she hated sick kids. In that case she
was not going to be a happy camper at Hope
House.

"Why did you pray that?" I asked.

"Oh, you know . . ." Courtney said. "It
would be embarrassing, like when my friends
come to visit," she explained. "It's embarrassing enough to be here myself, you know?"

"Oh, sure," I said breezily. "My friends come
visit me all the time too. So I'm glad to have a
normal roommate myself." I'm not sure why I
said this, since in reality I didn't have any
friends outside of Hope House. It's pretty hard
to make friends when you don't go to school.

"Oh, I'm so glad you're normal!" Courtney
cried with relief. She slipped her blond hair behind one ear and I noticed she had perfect little
diamond studs in her earlobes.

"There you are," said a voice from the doorway.

There stood an attractive middle-aged couple, impeccably dressed, if you go for that boring designer look. The woman looked remarkably like an older, darker version of Courtney, and the man had Courtney's beautiful blond hair.

"Ah, the parental units," I chirped. "Hi, I'm Star," I said cheerfully.

"Hello," the woman said, smiling at me distractedly and heading for Courtney as quick as her designer pumps could carry her. Her husband ambled more slowly, smiling kindly at me on his way across the room.

"Honey, I thought you came up early so you could lie down," Courtney's mom said in a strained voice. "Remember Dr. Steve said you should rest? You haven't even changed into your nightie!"

Courtney rolled her eyes. "I don't want to change, Mom."

"Well, at least lie down," her mother said, hovering over her.

"But I don't want to lie down," Courtney protested. She looked over at her father to back her up.

"You probably should, honey," her dad said mildly.

Courtney sighed and lay down on top of the

bedspread, folding her arms across her chest to let her mother know how much she hated it.

"That's better, sweetie," Courtney's mom said, stroking Courtney's perfect bangs out of her eyes. Courtney quickly brushed her bangs back down the way she wanted them. Her mother sighed and fiddled nervously with a gold earring.

"We saw Dr. Steve," Courtney's mom told her. "He said he'll be in after you have another EKG."

"Fine," Courtney said, as if she couldn't have cared less.

"I know you hate this, baby," her dad said softly, "but you have to follow the doctor's orders and rest, okay?"

"Okay," she agreed, smiling at her father. It was easy to see which parent was her favorite.

Courtney's mom kissed her on the forehead. "We'll be back first thing in the morning, sweetheart," she said. Courtney's father added his kiss. Courtney threw her arms around her father's neck and hugged him tight for a moment. "You'll be fine, baby," he assured her lovingly.

Courtney's dad smiled at me and her mother gave me a little "nice to meet you, dear" as they sailed out the door.

"I hate my mother," Courtney said casually, rolling her eyes.

"Well, of course," I agreed, knowing she didn't really mean it.

"If it was up to her I'd stay a child forever," Courtney moaned. "Seriously. She'd have me in frills and little patent leather party shoes if she could get away with it."

"Gross," I said sympathetically.

"She's worse than any of my friends' mothers," Courtney continued. "My friends always tease me about how naive I am. And it's all because my stupid mom barely lets me out of the house!" Courtney shook her head in disgust. "Is your mom like that too?" she asked.

"Not exactly. You'd have to meet Claudia to know what I mean."

"You call your mother Claudia?" she asked.

"It's her name," I said.

"Wow," Courtney breathed. She sat up against her pillows. "I can't believe my mother made me come here," she said. "My father didn't think it was necessary, but she always gets her way. I'm missing cheerleading practice and everything."

I tried to look casual. "You're a cheerleader?"

Courtney nodded. "Head cheerleader at South," she said proudly. "Hey, if we're the same age, how come I don't know you from school? Aren't you from Somerset?"

"I've been educated privately," I said loftily.

She wrinkled her perfect nose. "What does that mean?"

"You know, tutors. At home," I explained. "All us professionals do it that way."

"What are you talking about?" Courtney asked.

I shook my curls out of my face. I once saw a girl do that in this music video, and she looked very cool. "I'm an actress," I explained. "I have to be tutored privately so that when I'm in a show or a movie or a TV show, I don't miss school. The tutor just comes to the set with me."

Courtney stared at me, trying to decide if I was pulling her leg. "You aren't," she decided.

I just stared at her. After all, we professional actresses don't need to defend our careers, you know.

"Maybe you really are," she marveled, changing her mind. "Wait a minute, though. How could you be an actress in Somerset? I thought all the movies were made in Hollywood and all the plays were done in New York."

"That is why God created airplanes," I said.

Courtney didn't get it. She looked at me like I was crazy.

"To fly from Somerset to Hollywood or New York," I explained. So what if God had made her perfect looking. She clearly was not quick on the uptake.

She still couldn't decide whether to believe me or not.

"What have you ever been in?" she asked me cautiously.

"This and that," I said evasively, playing out the moment.

"Like what 'this and that'?" she asked, clearly back to believing I was a total liar.

"Did you ever see *The Hot House Princess*?" I asked casually, naming a low-budget movie that had become the biggest thing in the country about six months earlier. It was a movie about a girl from a small factory town who comes to New York to be a dancer. By day she auditions, and at night she's a waitress at the Hot House, the hippest club in New York. She starts a new dance craze at the club and then pretends she's a princess, because she's embarrassed by her real background. The dance from the movie, the Hot-Hot, had been adopted by people all over the country.

"I saw it four times with my best friend," Courtney said.

"I'm in it," I said calmly.

I was telling the truth.

Claudia knew the choreographer, who called her one day and asked her if she wanted to come back to New York and dance in the movie, for old times' sake. Naturally she had to take me with her. Fortunately I was going through a healthy period, and I'm a really good dancer. So there I was, bopping around on the set waiting for my mother, and my mom's friend the choreographer came over to me and said I was cute. Then he asked me if I wanted to be in the scene where the Hot House is turned over to the underage crowd, and the girl who stars in the movie has to wait on all the dancing teenyboppers. It was destiny.

In wardrobe they chose an acid-green miniskirt and crop top for me, which looked great with my copper-colored hair. Then a professional makeup lady put makeup on me. I spent two days dancing in that scene, which is actually about five minutes in the movie. But you can see me on the screen four different times. One time is from the back, but it's me. I ended up back in Hope House when we got home, with a bad pneumonia. I don't know if the dancing had anything to do with it, but even if it did, it was worth it.

"You aren't in that movie," Courtney said.

I told her the whole story. I might have embellished it a little—like I told her I had lunch one day with Jeff Howard, the hunky actor who played the male lead. Actually I had lunch in the same room with him, as did about three hundred other people. But this is a minor detail I didn't feel the need to go into.

Courtney stared at me, obviously impressed. "I never knew an actress before," she said.

I smiled benignly.

"Maybe it won't be so bad, being here," she added tentatively.

"Courtney Cambridge?" came a male voice from the door.

"That's me," Courtney said in a small voice.

A male attendant wheeled a machine over to her bed. She started to look scared again.

"EKG," he told her.

I knew what an EKG was. It was a test to measure how her heart was beating. They were going to put electrodes on her chest and get a readout that would show a line graph of beats. The test didn't hurt—I'd had it done once—but it was still scary. The attendant briskly pulled the curtains shut that divided our beds, to give her privacy.

"Star?" Courtney called from behind the curtain.

"What?" I called back.

"Will you keep talking to me while they do this test?" she asked me. "Is that all right?" she asked the attendant.

"It's okay," he said, "as long as you lie still."

"I will," she promised. "Star?" she called.

"Sure," I agreed.

As she lay there I told her all about *The Hot House Princess*, and all about moviemaking. I even told her I was up for a part in a series next fall. Well, actually, the choreographer had told me I was cute enough to be up for a part in a series that his friend was pitching, if his friend could ever get a deal. But that was close enough.

I just kept talking, because even if I wasn't sure I liked Courtney Cambridge, I knew how it felt to be scared. I just hoped my story was riveting enough to take her mind off the machine she was attached to, measuring beat after beat of her injured heart.

3

The attendant opened Courtney's curtains with a flourish and rolled the EKG machine out of the room.

"That wasn't so bad," Courtney said in a small voice. "At least it didn't hurt."

I nodded. "It's one of the few things they can do to you here that really, truly doesn't," I said. "You have to learn their codes. For example, if they say, 'It won't hurt a bit,' that means, 'This is going to hurt quite a bit, but I'm trying to get you to be cooperative.' If they say, 'You'll feel some discomfort,' it means they're going to kill you."

"I'll remember," Courtney said shakily. She got up and unzipped the small suitcase her dad had left by her bed. "You seem to know a lot about this," Courtney added, pulling out a gorgeous white cotton-and-lace nightgown with pink ribbon trimming. "Have you been at Hope House before?"

"Once or twice," I said. "Hey, great nightgown," I added, eager to change the subject. "It looks like it cost a mint."

"I hate it," Courtney said, making a face. "I wanted to just bring my long T-shirts, that's what I sleep in. Mom said it wasn't appropriate. She bought me this ugly thing this morning."

"Hey, who's sick here, you or your mother?" I asked. "I say wear what you want."

"No one would care?" she asked.

"Trust me, no one at Hope House is real big on fashion," I said wryly.

"Good," she said. "Then I'm not wearing it." She held it up and looked over at me. "Here," she said impetuously. "You take it." She handed me the nightgown and before I could say anything, she disappeared into the bathroom to change into her long T-shirt.

Wow. That nightgown was really beautiful. I hadn't expected Courtney to turn out to be a generous person. Maybe I was judging her too quickly. Maybe we were really going to be friends.

Courtney came out of the bathroom looking comfortable in a T-shirt that read PROPERTY OF INDIANA STATE. I was just about to thank her for the nightgown when there was a knock on the door.

"Courtney?"

"Julie!" Courtney cried. "I can't believe you're here!"

Julie ran over to Courtney and hugged her hard. I took in her bouncy brown hair tied back with a maroon ribbon, and the maroon-and-white short, pleated skirt and sweater set that marked her as a South Somerset Middle School cheerleader.

"Oh, did I hurt you?" Julie asked Courtney as she quickly stopped hugging her.

"I'm not breakable, you idiot," Courtney said happily. "I'm so glad you're here. Can you believe I'm in this prison?"

"Bogus," Julie agreed. She sat down next to Courtney on her bed. "You look, like, normal," she said.

"I am normal," Courtney said.

"Yeah, it's this place that isn't," I quipped from my bed.

All of a sudden Courtney remembered I was in the room. "Oh, Julie, this is my roommate, Star. Star, this is my best friend, Julie."

"Hi," Julie said, smiling in my direction. I smiled back, but she immediately returned her attention to Courtney. "Listen, I can only stay a minute. I had to sneak out of cheerleading practice and run all the way over here."

"Wow, Lundgren will kill you," Courtney said.

"Oh, well, you're worth it," Julie said, grinning at her friend. "This place is, like, seriously creepy," Julie added. "Did you see that bald kid walking around with that big thing hooked up to his arm?" she asked with a shudder.

"I saw him," Courtney said grimly. A thought struck her and she grabbed the sleeve of Julie's sweater. "Who knows I'm here?" she demanded.

"No one," Julie said. "I mean, just me. You told me last night you might have to come here, and then when I called after lunch and you weren't home—" Julie began.

"Besides you," Courtney interrupted impatiently. "Does Jeff know? Because I will die if Jeff knows I'm here."

"He doesn't. Everyone at school is talking, because you've been out so long. I just said you had a bad flu."

Courtney grabbed Julie's sleeve again. "You won't tell?" she begged.

"Of course I won't tell, you idiot," Julie said. "My mom knows, though, because your mom told her. And you know my mother—"

"—has the biggest mouth on the planet,"

Courtney groaned, finishing Julie's sentence for her. "I'm doomed."

"I told her not to tell," Julie said. "I'll tell her again."

"Make her promise," Courtney said.

"I will," Julie assured her. She looked Courtney over again. "So you're really okay and everything?"

"Yes, I'm fine. I don't even feel sick. This is my mother's fault, you know." Courtney narrowed her eyes. "I bet she did it to try and keep me from the dance next month."

"Your mom didn't exactly make you sick," Julie said.

"Oh, you know what I mean," Courtney said. "You know how she overreacts to everything. Well, it won't work. I'm not missing my very first date with Jeff for anything in the world."

"I know you won't," Julie said with a grin. "Oh, I got the most awesome outfit to wear. The skirt is, like, totally indecent!"

"I can't wait to see it," Courtney said.

"Listen, I gotta run before Loudmouth Lundgren realizes I'm gone," Julie said, getting up from Courtney's bed. "She'll have a kitten. My theory is she's just ticked because she got old and fat. Can you believe she was ever a cheerleader?"

"Can you see her turning a cartwheel?" Courtney asked. They both cracked up.

"Okay, gotta boogie," Julie said, hugging Courtney. "So I'll see you soon," she promised. "Good thing I'm a fast runner!" she added as she sprinted out the door.

"Nice girl, very chatty, slightly hyper," I commented after Julie disappeared out the door.

"Julie is my best friend in the entire world," Courtney said.

"I guess you have tons of friends," I said.

"Yeah, tons," Courtney agreed.

"Yeah, me too," I said casually.

"So, do you have a boyfriend?" Courtney asked, pulling her knees up under her T-shirt.

"Oh, sure, I have tons of those too," I said breezily.

She looked at me. "You've got tons of boyfriends?"

"Yeah, actors," I said knowingly.

"I only have one," Courtney said. "I guess he's my boyfriend—I mean, I think he's my boyfriend. His name is Jeff Lowell. He invited me to our school's dance next month. Does that make him my boyfriend?"

"Depends," I told her. "Was he asking you because he likes you, or was he asking you with an ulterior motive?"

"Like what?" she asked, her eyebrows knitted together with anxiety.

I shrugged. "Oh, let's see . . . to make someone else jealous, because his mother made him . . ."

Courtney looked horrified. "He wouldn't do that. Would he?"

I shrugged again. "Hard to say. I once played the part of a girl who only pretends to like this guy because she's really in love with his older brother," I said. "At first he doesn't even know she's alive, but then he falls madly, passionately in love with her. . . ."

Now Courtney was starting to panic. "But Jeff doesn't even have an older brother!"

I winced. "No need to be so literal," I explained.

Courtney bit her lower lip. She really looked upset. At first I felt good, which only shows that at times I am not a very nice human being. But then I started to feel kind of guilty. I decided to let her off the hook.

"Listen, you don't need to worry," I told her. "That was made up. It came from some artist's imagination. I'm sure he really likes you."

"I don't know," she said, her voice now full of doubt. She was still chewing on her lower lip. "Maybe the person that wrote this thing really knows. Maybe it was based on real life. What was it, a movie?"

I shook my head.

"A play?" she asked.

"Sort of," I qualified.

"What does 'sort of' mean?"

"A scene from a play," I explained.

"So who wrote it?"

"I sort of did," I confessed.

"Where was it performed?" she asked.

"Here," I admitted.

I expected her to laugh at me, but she didn't.

"Wow, that's great. You write and act. You're really talented," she marveled.

"Oh, well, I still have a lot to learn," I assured her.

Sure, now I could afford to be humble.

"And you just made the whole thing up from your head?" she asked me. "I wish I could do that!"

"It takes a lot of practice," I told her.

"So where do you get your ideas?"

"Life," I answered with a broad sweep of my arm.

Her eyes got wider. "You mean you actually fell in love with the older brother of one of your boyfriends?"

I nodded, getting carried away with my own

story. "And the really awful thing is"—I paused dramatically—"he's right here in Hope House this very minute!"

"No!" Courtney gasped.

"Yes!" I said dramatically. "He's in 2-B!" I remembered that Sally had mentioned a cute guy was in that room.

Okay, okay. Right now you are saying to yourself, "This girl is a total liar." I mean, you know as well as I do that I didn't even know the guy in 2-B. But I prefer to term it the fine art of exaggeration. We creative geniuses do this sort of thing a lot.

"Omigosh, what are you going to do?" Courtney gasped, completely forgetting about her own situation with Jeff.

Before I could invent an answer, I heard the unmistakable sounds of Ms. Tortunesky's footsteps clomping down the hall toward my room. The nurses wore crepe-soled shoes that moved silently around Hope House. The doctors and other workers wore whatever kind of shoes they wanted to wear. Only The Torturer wore heavy lace-up army boots, whose clunking sound ominously preceded her every arrival.

"Quick! Run for your life!" I screamed, throwing the pillow over my head.

"Good afternoon," Ms. Tortunesky barked, marching over to my bed.

"What's so good about it?" I mumbled from underneath my pillow.

I felt the giant hand of The Torturer lift the pillow from my head.

"So, I haven't seen you in three months," Ms. Tortunesky remarked. "Now that you're back we have plenty of work to do." She began to briskly arrange the pillows on the bed for my torture.

I looked over at Courtney. She was staring at Ms. Tortunesky as if she were looking at a Martian in combat boots.

"Now, Ms. Tortunesky, where are your manners?" I chided her. "This is my roommate, Courtney Cambridge, and this is the one and only Ms. Tortunesky," I said, introducing them.

"Hello," Courtney said in a small voice.

"You don't have cystic fibrosis, correct?" Ms. Tortunesky shot at Courtney.

"Oh, no," Courtney assured her. She was staring at me and The Torturer as if we were the stars of a horror movie.

"No need to stare, young lady," Ms. Tortunesky snapped at Courtney, who practically jumped out of her bed with fright. Ms. Tortunesky pulled the curtain shut around my bed for privacy and put the oxygen mask on my face. After I had taken several breaths of Mucomyst, she turned to me. "Assume the position, please!" she ordered.

I knew Courtney did not have a clue as to what was going on. The curtain hadn't shut completely, and as I turned over to get myself set up on the pillows I could see Courtney's face peering at me anxiously through the curtain's opening.

I waved at her. "Know any good dirty jokes?" I asked.

Ms. Tortunesky whipped around and marched back to the curtain, pulling it shut more briskly this time. The curtain obstinately pulled back on the runner so that Courtney still had a clear view.

"Might as well give up," I told Ms. Tortunesky cheerfully. "Courtney is going to witness your crime."

"That's enough levity," The Torturer snapped. "We have work to do."

"Watch closely," I called to Courtney through the opening in the curtain. I moved around so that the pillows were correctly positioned under me. "You are about to see a thirteen-year-old girl whacked to death."

Courtney looked so freaked out that I winked

at her, then I turned my head so that I faced the other side of the room. I didn't want Courtney to see the fear on my face as The Torturer raised her huge fist for the first blow.

4

"This is the best chicken I ever tasted in my life," Courtney said, licking her fingers.

"Have some more," I offered, holding the barrel of fried chicken bits out to her. She took three more and popped one in her mouth.

"Mmmmm, heaven." Courtney sighed.

It was right after dinner—which we hadn't gone down to the dining room to eat. It turned out that Courtney didn't have any dietary restrictions either. So when Ms. McG. came to take me to the treatment room to have my IV needle put in (this is how they drip antibiotics into my arm), I gave her a pitiful look and asked if Courtney and I could both eat in my room. Ms. McG. is a real softie. She said yes.

"Hey, she's eating my chicken!" Sally protested from the doorway.

"Oops," said Courtney, midbite.

"Hey, Sally, it's called sharing," I admonished her.

Sally marched over to Courtney and picked up three chicken bits. She popped all three into her mouth at once, which was seriously gross.

"Sally, sweetie, Daddy and I want to spend time with you before beddy-bye," Sally's mother called from the door.

"Oh, Mother," Sally whined through her mouthful of chicken. She scuffed her way across the room to the door.

"Beddy-bye?" Courtney mouthed to me. I stifled a laugh.

"Here, Sally, take your ice cream," I offered, handing it to her. It was the least I could do for a girl whose mother was so excruciating.

Courtney eyed the IV that was stuck in my arm. "Does it hurt?" she asked tentatively.

"Sometimes," I told her truthfully.

"It looks horrible," she said, making a face. It was the same face she'd made when she talked about seeing the bald kid in the hall.

"It looks worse than it is," I assured her. No way was I going to be lumped in her mind with those really sick kids. "No problem, I'm used to it," I added breezily. I took one of Aunt Amy's chocolate desserts out of the huge picnic basket that she'd brought the food over in. It was a little awkward to do with one arm, since I hated to use the one with the IV stuck in it for fear I'd dislodge the needle and they'd have to start all over again. "So, are you ready to taste the greatest thing you ever tasted in your life?" I asked her, handing her a dessert.

She took the towering heap of dark chocolate and whipped cream and spooned some into her mouth. "I think I just died and went to heaven," she said, her eyes closed in bliss.

Dr. Steve and Andrea walked into the room at the same time.

"I smell pizza!" Dr. Steve said, happily heading for the pizza box.

"How was the *M* food?" I asked them wickedly.

"I pushed it around on my plate politely and then headed right back up here," Andrea said, lifting a slice of pizza.

"Hi, Star, long time no see!" came a voice from the door. It belonged to Rusty Feller. He's a nurse who works part-time at Hope House. He is one of the skinniest human beings I've ever seen. He's totally nerdy looking. He has bright red hair, lots of freckles, and he is a complete klutz. He's also a great guy—I mean, really great—the kind of person you want for your friend when life gets rough.

"Yeah, food!" Rusty cheered. It's amazing, but as skinny as Rusty is, he absolutely loves to eat. He headed for the pizza box but tripped over something invisible on the floor and landed on his behind. "Wow! Dangerous!" Rusty said, staring at the floor as if it were covered with oil. He ran his hand through his red hair and it stood straight on end.

I had just started to introduce Rusty to Courtney, when Alison Kim came in hand-in-hand with Alex Fury. Alison is sixteen and very bubbly. Normally I can't stand bubbly, but she's so sincere that it makes it all right. She sings and plays the guitar—she's the kind of girl who likes to organize sing-alongs. She's been a volunteer at Hope House ever since her little sister, Mary, was here for her Hodgkin's disease. Mary died two years ago. Alison never talks about it.

Alex is a seven-year-old kid with kidney disease. He comes in three times a week for dialysis. Everyone knows he needs a kidney transplant or he might die. He's a really cute kid—I've known him for years. He knows everything there is to know about basketball, which he will talk about endlessly if you give him the chance. Personally basketball strikes me as a game where a bunch of pituitary cases in satin underwear chase a ball around, so I try to steer the kid to other topics.

Word of the goodies in my room spread like

wildfire. Dr. Ambrose came in, smiling this great smile she has. You should see her—she looks like a toothpaste ad, but in a good way. She's a resident in pediatrics, meaning she takes care of kids. She has glossy chestnut-colored hair and almond-shaped green eyes. She wears a lot of silk dresses that are tasteful without being obnoxious.

There is a big rumor going around that she and Dr. Graham have the hots for each other. Dr. Graham is a psychologist and the head of Hope House. I heard his wife died of leukemia a long time ago, and he always seems a little sad to me. However, I have noticed that whenever Dr. Ambrose is around he perks up considerably. I've also noticed that he manages to show up wherever she shows up. And then he acts really nervous around her, which is quite funny, considering the fact that he's a shrink.

Just as Dr. Ambrose was splitting a second slice of pizza with Andrea, wouldn't you know that Dr. Graham would amble into my room. He smiled at me and said hello, but I could see his eyes were really searching the room for Dr. Ambrose. When he actually caught her eye, he kind of blushed and looked away. In my opinion it is hilarious to see grown-ups acting like fools when they get hit with the love bug. I intend never to be reduced to this state.

Before I knew it everyone was eating and laughing and a huge party was going on in my room. Sally snuck back in after her parental units left, and even Rachel Harris made her way to my room.

Rachel is fifteen. She was admitted for the first time during my last admission about three months ago. She pretty much stayed in her room and didn't mix with anyone. Whenever I did see her, she always had her hair and nails and clothes absolutely perfect, which no one else at Hope House cares about. It was very bizarre to see this kind of perfection, because no matter what Rachel did, she looked horrid. This is because she has anorexia, and she's so skinny, she looks like she's barely alive. But no matter how thin Rachel gets, she looks in the mirror and sees this cow looking back at her. Naturally Rachel didn't eat any of the food— she had an IV in her arm that was feeding her a high-calorie liquid. I noticed her hair was thinner than the last time I'd seen her.

It was hard for me to feel very friendly toward Rachel. She's one of those people who always know better. Also, although I've never seen her eat anything, she wants to talk about food all the time. She cuts recipes out of magazines. Now, tell me that isn't weird. Still, the very fact that she came to my room meant she was making progress—socially, at least.

After everyone had stuffed their faces and Rusty had managed to stab his finger with his penknife and poke himself in the eye with a straw, Alison decided it was "kum ba yah" time. Maybe you've never heard of "Kum Ba Yah." It's this folk song from the Stone Age or something that Alison's mom taught her. The song keeps repeating the line "Kum ba yah, my Lord, kum ba yah." Everyone is supposed to sing along. Being a girl who likes to know what I'm singing about, I asked Alison what "kum ba yah" means. She didn't know. I've asked everybody who knows this stupid song, and no one knows what it means, yet everyone is perfectly willing to sing it. So I've decided it means doggie doo. Imagine a roomful of people singing, "Doggie doo, my Lord, doggie doo." This is why I refuse to sing this stupid song.

While Alison sprinted to the rec room to get her guitar, I told Courtney about the true meaning of "kum ba yah." Wouldn't you know it was the first song Alison played. Courtney and I laughed so hard throughout the song that I actually had to run to the bathroom or I would have peed my pants. Poor Rusty figured we were laughing at him, and he kept checking to see if he had food on his teeth or if his fly was unzipped.

We were all having such a good time that at first no one noticed that Sally was acting weird. She stood up and kind of weaved around the room as if someone had spiked her milk. I figured she was trying to get attention in her usual lame way. It happened in just a couple of seconds—first she was stumbling, and the next thing I knew she was lying on the ground, her eyes rolling back in her head, jerking her arms and legs around horribly. Dr. Ambrose jumped up and ran out of the room, then ran back in in a flash with a hypodermic needle in her hand. She quickly injected Sally as we all stood around helplessly.

"She'll be fine in a minute," Dr. Ambrose assured us. "She's in insulin shock. I've given her something to raise her blood sugar level."

Courtney had her hand clamped over her mouth in horror. She looked like she was forcing herself not to cry. Alex Fury held tightly to Rusty's hand. He didn't say a word. He'd seen too many horrible, scary things happen to kids at Hope House. This was just one more.

Sally came around in a few minutes, and Dr. Ambrose helped her back to her room. After that no one felt much like partying anymore. Maybe we could forget for a while that the possibility of death always hung around Hope House, but we could never forget for long. Life just wouldn't let us.

As if Sally's seizure hadn't been bad enough, when I looked up from throwing the pizza box in the garbage, there stood The Torturer. I had actually forgotten about thumps. The presence of Ms. Tortunesky would kill any party, but the spirit in the room had fizzled, anyway.

"It's time for her therapy," Ms. Tortunesky announced. She pointed to me as she said "her." This was because she refuses to call me Star, which she insists is not the name God and my parents gave me. However, the one time she called me Stella I managed to by-mistake-on-purpose cough up all my phlegm on her. I grant you it was disgusting, but it did the trick.

Oh, no, another session of her horrible thumps. The very thought of it made my stomach queasy and I broke out in a sweat. It felt like everyone in the room was staring at me, feeling sorry for me, just like they felt sorry for Sally. I hated that more than anything in the world.

"Hey, Ms. Tortunesky, I had no idea you were such a party animal!" I called out to her. I sounded like I didn't have a care in the world, which is exactly how I wanted to sound.

She remained stone faced.

"I think she's ticked because we didn't save her any dessert," I confided to Courtney. Courtney was still too weirded out about what had happened to Sally and too intimidated by The Torturer to say anything. She just gulped.

Everyone left quickly. Even Dr. Graham seemed to be intimidated by The Torturer. He patted my hand, said, "Nice party," and skedaddled out of my room with everyone else. Well, who could blame them—I would have left, too, if I could have. I was still hurting from her afternoon thumps.

The Torturer drew the curtain shut around my bed and slapped the oxygen mask on my face. I wasn't ready. A strange thing happened. All of a sudden I felt like I couldn't breathe. I pulled the mask off and gulped at the air. The Torturer snapped it back in place.

"I can't breathe!" I told her, pulling it off again.

The Torturer's face changed. "Are you congested? Do you feel it in your lungs?" she asked quickly.

"No, no, it's just . . ." I couldn't explain.

She stared at me. "You just want to shirk what you know has to be done," she decided. She slapped the mask back on me. This time I was okay. I breathed in the Mucomyst like a good girl. In my mind something else was happening. All the time I was breathing, I was strangling the ugly neck of The Torturer.

She pounded and pounded—it seemed to go on forever. Two thumps a day had been bad enough. I didn't see how I could possibly live through three. When she finished I was completely exhausted. My hair was stuck to my sweaty face and I felt really disgusting. Ms. Tortunesky looked quite satisfied. She nodded at me briskly and opened the curtain with a flourish. I could feel Courtney's eyes on me, but I just lay there with my eyes closed, willing The Torturer to leave. She finally did, announcing that she would see me in the morning at six A.M.

"Star?" Courtney whispered. "Are you okay?"

"Sure she's okay," came a throaty voice from the door. It was my mother. "My girl's always okay, right?" she asked me.

"Sure," I said, struggling to sit up. "No problem," I added.

I guess I should explain about my mother and me. I really like Claudia, and Claudia really likes me, but Claudia does not like my disease. I think maybe it scares her too much, which scares me too much, so we never talk about it. I always act like it's no big thing, and she always acts like she believes me. This is just the way it is.

"That's my girl," Claudia said approvingly, kissing my cheek. She fell into the chair nearest my bed. She looked flushed and pretty in a pair of jeans and an old sweatshirt. She definitely did not look like anyone's mom.

"You should have seen the new ballet class I had tonight," my mom said, rolling her eyes. "It was a new low in the art form." One of my mom's classes at her dance school was Adult Beginners Ballet. Claudia found it unbearable. She glanced over at Courtney and gave her a friendly wave. "Hi, I'm Star's mom," she said. "Call me Claudia."

"Okay, Claudia," Courtney said, trying out the sound of my mother's first name. "I'm Courtney."

"So what's happening?" my mom asked casually.

I shrugged. "The usual," I said, as if nothing bothered me.

Claudia smiled at me. "You're such a trouper," she said. She opened her purse and pulled out a hard candy, unwrapped it, and popped it in her mouth. "This is supposed to help me not want cigarettes," she explained to Courtney.

"Is it working?" Courtney asked politely.

"No," Claudia told her. "I still crave cigarettes, only now I've gained five pounds from the stupid candy."

"You teach dance, right?" Courtney asked.

"You got it," Claudia said.

"I always wanted to study ballet," Courtney said. "I'm a cheerleader now," she added proudly.

"Oh, cool. Well, we'll work something out when you get out of here, okay?" Claudia said.

"That would be great!" Courtney agreed.

Claudia stayed about a half hour, regaling us with funny stories about her dance classes. Finally she looked at her watch and scrambled out of her chair.

"Gotta run, I'm expecting a big call from New York tonight," she told us, "and I do mean big."

"A part?" I asked her with excitement.

She smiled. "I don't want to jinx it by talking about it," she said.

"On Broadway?" I asked. "Off-Broadway?"

Claudia laughed. "Let's just say that I better keep these dancing legs in primo shape," she said. "Okay, sleep well, sweetie, I'll see you tomorrow." Claudia kissed me on the top of my sweaty head. "Hey, nice meeting you," she called to Courtney. "We'll work out something with the lessons!"

"Your mother is unbelievably fabulous," Courtney told me after Claudia left.

"I know," I said.

"Why couldn't my father have married someone like her?" Courtney asked plaintively.

"Because then there'd be no you," I pointed out in a tired voice. I really was feeling exhausted. Sometimes being perky for Claudia took its toll.

Courtney hugged her knees to her chest. "You know, I thought this would be awful—that being here would be the worst thing that could happen to me," she confessed. "But it's really okay. I guess maybe they put us together because we're not really as sick as the others," Courtney said.

"Probably," I agreed. I was too tired to say much of anything else.

Courtney got her toothbrush and toothpaste out of her suitcase, and headed for the bathroom. "I'm really glad you're my roommate," she said in a shy voice.

"It's gonna be a riot," I assured her as she closed the bathroom door.

I stared at the ceiling. So we were going to be friends. Maybe we could even stay friends after Courtney got out and went home. It had never happened before. I'd had roommates that had said we'd stay friends, but as soon as they'd gotten out of Hope House, they'd forgotten all about me. Not that I blamed them. Who would want to be reminded of a place where everyone was sick, where some kids actually died? But maybe Courtney was different. Maybe it was possible.

And all I had to do to keep her as my friend was to spend twenty-four hours a day pretending that I wasn't really very sick at all.

No problem.

5

"Pssst, Sally!" I hissed at her outside of the recreation room. "What did you find out?"

It was Saturday, two weeks later, and I had sent Sally on a mission. I needed to find out whatever I could about the mystery guy in 2-B. Because of me and my big mouth, Courtney thought I was madly in love with whoever was lying in that bed. She'd been asking me about him for the past two weeks. I had come up with a zillion excuses as to why she couldn't meet him, and why he never came to our room. Even my fertile imagination was starting to get overtaxed. I had to get some info on him and I had to get it fast. Courtney had this plan that we should go visit him in his room so she could learn more about how to handle men. Of course she thought I was an expert.

"Well, he hasn't come down to any meals, no one knows much about him," Sally told me.

"I already know that," I said impatiently. "Did you find out anything or not?"

"Maybe I did and maybe I didn't," she answered cagily.

"You did!" I cried. I could read Sally like a book.

"Why should I help you, anyway?" Sally whined. "You don't seem to have time for anyone but your stuck-up roommate."

"She's not stuck-up," I told Sally. Sally had one of her poor-me looks on her face. I had to think quickly. "Say, I've got an idea," I told Sally. "Why don't you come over to our room for dinner tonight? I'll call Aunt Amy and get some incredible stuff!"

"Really?" Sally asked, her face lighting up. "I mean, I guess," she added, trying to pretend she didn't care all that much.

"Great!" I told her. "Now tell me about the guy."

"Well, his name is Tom Levine. He's fifteen," Sally said.

"So far, so good," I encouraged her.

"He's from Carver City," she said, naming a town about fifty miles from Somerset. "He's about five eight, he has brown hair and blue eyes, and he's captain of his school's junior varsity tennis team.''

"Wow, Sally, how did you find out all of that?" I asked her. "I'm impressed."

Sally shrugged. "Alison. I pumped her while I pretended to learn some guitar chords."

"You're a good friend," I told Sally. At the moment I said it, I even believed it. "So why doesn't this Tom guy ever come out of his room?"

"That I don't know," Sally answered. "But Alison said Tom was really cute, and she also said he was really sad." She shrugged.

"Thanks, Sally, I owe you one," I told her, rushing back toward my room as quickly as I could with the stupid IV pole wheeling with me.

"I'm still invited for dinner, right?" she called to me.

"Sure!" I called back, disappearing around the corner.

When I got back to my room, Courtney's friend Julie was sitting on Courtney's bed. Courtney was holding her hands over her face.

"This can't be happening!" she moaned. "My life is ruined!"

"I'm really sorry," Julie said, "but you know my mother. She can't keep her mouth shut!"

"What happened?" I asked.

"Julie's mom is friends with Jeff's mom, and she told her I was in here. Jeff's mom told Jeff, and then Jeff told Julie he's coming to visit me tonight after dinner!"

"So that means he really likes you," I told her. "That's not so terrible."

Courtney stared at me. "Don't you understand? I don't want him to visit me here! It's not like I'm getting my tonsils out or something."

"But you look normal," Julie said.

"Everyone knows normal kids don't come to this place." Courtney sighed.

Julie got up from Courtney's bed. "I'm really sorry," she told Courtney again. "I'd kill my mom for you, if I thought I could get away with it."

"At least you warned me," Courtney said.

"I gotta go, my mom is waiting in the car downstairs," Julie said. "She wanted to come in with me, but I begged her to wait in the car."

"Well, thanks for that, anyway," Courtney said.

"I'll come back tomorrow," Julie promised. "Can Evelyn and Beth and Stacey come?" she asked. "They want to."

"Sure," Courtney said. "Now that Jeff knows, it doesn't matter."

Julie waved good-bye cheerfully and ran out the door.

"He's never going to want to take me to the dance after he sees me in this place," Courtney moaned.

"Sure he will," I told her.

"You don't understand," Courtney said. "I don't know how to talk to him, even in school. It's horrible! Everyone thinks that just because I'm a cheerleader I must be really cool around boys, but I'm not."

"They're just people," I told her.

"No, they're not, they're boys," she said. "I'm not like you—I wish I could be. It was hard enough acting normal around him in school. Seeing him here . . . well, I'll just die!"

She really did look upset, but my mind was stuck on that "I wish I could be like you" remark. Courtney Cambridge wanted to be like me? Of course, that was only because she didn't know me very well yet. But so what? That meant I was an even greater actress than I had given myself credit for being. Just as I was musing over this, Dr. Steve bounded cheerfully into the room.

"How are my two favorite girls today?" he asked us.

"I'm fine. Courtney's life is ruined," I answered cheerfully.

"What's wrong?" Dr. Steve asked, taking a chair by Courtney's bed.

Courtney just groaned, so I answered for her. "Her boyfriend is coming to visit," I explained.

"Well, that's nice," Dr. Steve said, clearly missing the larger picture. He fiddled with a pen in the pocket of his jacket and looked at Courtney. "We're going to start you on some intravenous antibiotics today, Courtney. I think it will help you get better faster."

Courtney looked at him in alarm. "Wait a second. Are you telling me that you're going to stick one of those things in my arm like Star has?" she asked in horror.

"It looks much worse than it actually feels," Dr. Steve assured her.

"So when does this happen?" Courtney asked nervously.

"The nurse will take you into the blood room and hook you up in about an hour," Dr. Steve said. "I just wanted to stop in and explain. It's the same antibiotics you've been taking orally."

"So why do I have to switch, then?" Courtney asked plaintively.

"Intravenous medication is much more efficient," he told her. "It won't be so bad. And I think we'll see a big improvement in a few days." He patted her hand.

Courtney lay down on her pillows after Dr. Steve left and stared at the ceiling. "Jeff is going to see me hooked up to that thing. I can't stand it," she moaned. "I will look like a complete idiot. I won't be able to say one word to him, it will be so mortifying." She sighed a giant sigh. "At least your boyfriend is in here with you." She sighed again. "Why won't you tell me what's wrong with him?"

"With Tom? He's, um . . . it's kind of complicated," I managed.

"Is he embarrassed? Is that why you keep going into his room by yourself?" she asked.

Okay, so I lied. I told Courtney I was going to visit my beloved, then I'd walk around the halls for a while and circle back to our room. It wasn't too hard to fool her. Courtney was very tired and Dr. Steve encouraged her to get all the bed rest she could.

"Yep, he's embarrassed, all right," I agreed. "See, he's this big tennis player, and, um, he's not used to being sick."

"Yeah, well, I can relate to that," Courtney said morosely. She shook her head. "I can't believe Jeff is coming here. This is absolutely the worst day of my life."

"It can't be that bad," I told her.

"It is," she insisted. "I know it wouldn't be for you, you can talk to anybody. You're an actress. But I can't! I just can't!"

Maybe the great idea occurred to me because Courtney seemed to think I was capable of one. But I knew it was fabulous as soon as it popped into my head. "I'm brilliant!" I cried.

"I know," she mumbled, "but I'm not."

"No, really, I just got this incredible idea!" I told her. "I'll write a scene based on you and Jeff, set right here in this room. I'll figure out exactly what you should say and how you should act. Then you'll be completely prepared when he shows up!"

Her face showed some interest. "You can do that?"

"Of course I can do that!" I cried. "I can do anything!"

Courtney sat up and stared at me. "But what about the IV?"

"We'll work that in," I assured her. "It's all in how you present it. Attitude is everything," I explained. I grabbed some paper and a pen from the nightstand. "Okay, we need a script. Let's see, I need to know more about Jeff," I told her.

Courtney told me all about the guy. He sounded wonderful. He was a really good athlete and he got good grades and according to

Courtney he was the cutest guy in her class. I certainly didn't know any guys like that. But then, I didn't know any guys at all.

Just when Courtney was winding down in her rhapsody about Jeff, Ms. McG. came by to take Courtney to the blood room.

"I guess I have to," Courtney said. She looked scared.

"It's really not so bad. I promise," I told her.

Fortunately Courtney had good veins, and it wasn't long before she made her way back to our room, dragging the pole that dripped clear liquid antibiotics into her arm. Her face looked pale, but other than that she seemed okay.

"Okay, I made a few notes while you were gone," I said, waving my pad at her. "I say we go for the scared-but-brave approach."

"What's that?" she asked me, perched on the edge of her bed.

"What do all great heroines have in common?" I asked. "Bravery!"

"Bravery?" she echoed uncertainly.

"Bravery. Guys love that," I assured her. "First we have to figure out your look. Pale is good," I said, eyeing her closely. "We'll go with pale, meaning no Pan-Cake."

"Pancake?" she repeated. "What do pancakes have to do with anything?"

"It's a kind of face makeup that we professional actors use," I explained. "But in this case we want that naturally pale look, so skip the blush."

"Right," she said seriously. "What else?"

"A touch of mascara," I decided, "and the tiniest bit of pink lipstick." I eyed her critically. Even after two weeks at Hope House her perfect hair still looked perfect. "A long braid," I said, nodding. "Very old-fashioned."

"Yuck!" Courtney said.

"Old-fashioned is good. Modern bravery, old-fashioned virtue, it'll work like a charm," I said. I grabbed her hairbrush from the nightstand.

"I don't know about this. . . ." she said.

"Okay, if you don't want my expert help, you're on your own," I said, pretending I was ready to put the brush down.

"No, no, I'm desperate," she told me. "Do the braid."

It turned out a little messy, because of my IV, but Courtney was so gorgeous and her hair was so pretty that she looked great, anyway. We got out her mascara and lipstick, and she applied them carefully. Fortunately she was right-handed and her IV was in her left arm.

"Perfect," I decided. "Now we need to improvise the script."

"What do you mean, improvise?" she asked.

I sighed. It's so difficult to work with amateurs.

"Make up the dialogue, pretend I'm him and you're you," I instructed her.

"I feel like an idiot," Courtney said.

I put my hands on my hips. "Courtney, I'm doing this for you," I reminded her. "Who is the experienced one here?"

"Okay, okay," she said, relenting. "What do I do?"

"I'm Jeff. I'm walking into the room," I said, heading for the door. I went outside, then came back in. "Hi, Courtney," I said in a really deep voice. "How delightful to see you."

Courtney looked at me like I was crazy. "How delightful to see you? If Jeff was lame enough to say, 'How delightful to see you,' would I be going out with him?" she asked me.

"Okay, my early drafts are sometimes a little stilted," I said. "I'll try again." I walked out the door. Then I stood there and tried to figure out what an incredibly cool, popular thirteen-year-old guy would say to an incredibly cool, popular thirteen-year-old girl that he really liked. I mean, let's face it, I had absolutely no frame of reference. I had to think fast. Aha! I could make it kind of like the incredibly cool, popular guy in *The Hot House Princess*, only younger.

I swaggered into the room. "Yo, babe, how

you doing?" I asked Courtney, heading for her side of the room.

"Oh, hi, Jeff," Courtney said. "I am fine. How are you?"

For the record, Courtney was not a born actress. In fact, she was frightening. I pressed on.

"So, babe, what's the deal? You got the flu or what?" I bellowed.

Courtney looked disgusted. "Star, Jeff doesn't have a New York accent."

Oops. The incredibly cool guy in *Hot House Princess* had a New York accent.

"Listen, Courtney, the first rule of improvisation is you never break character. Meaning, I am Jeff, so don't call me Star."

I closed my eyes to concentrate. I had seen a real actress who had five lines in *Hot House Princess* do this. It was very impressive looking.

"Babe, what can I do to make you feel better?" I growled in my Jeff voice.

Courtney looked stumped.

"Tell him, 'Oh, nothing, I'll be fine,' in a tortured tone of voice," I whispered at her.

"Oh, nothing, I'll be fine," she said with a sigh.

"You're so brave," I said, rushing to her side.

"I have to be strong," Courtney said. "For my father. He'll worry," she added dramatically.

So far, so good. She was finally getting the hang of it.

I took her hand in mine. "Will you be better in time for the dance, babe?" I asked her.

"Oh, yes," she said.

"If not, I'll understand," I told her. "And I'll think about you all night."

"You mean you'd go without me?" Courtney asked, trying to sustain her brave-and-noble voice.

"Yes, but I wouldn't have fun," I promised solemnly.

"What would you do, dance with that pig Janis Larski?" Courtney asked.

"No, I—"

"You probably would," Courtney interrupted me. "I know she likes you. You'll probably go to the dance with her. Your mother will probably make you!" Courtney yelled. "And all because I'm stuck in this stupid place with this stupid thing in my stupid arm!"

This was not going at all well.

"Uh, gee, Courtney," I said.

"It's no use, Star," Courtney wailed. "I can't do this. I can't talk to him. Either I can't say anything at all, or else I say something totally dweeby. I'm hopeless."

"Maybe it would work if I wrote out all the

lines for you, and you memorized them," I suggested.

"I'd just forget what I was supposed to say," she told me. She really did look miserable. "It would be so much easier if he were here as a patient, like Tom." She sighed. "If he could just get a little sick for a little while, and then we could both get better and go to the dance." Courtney sat back up and stared at me. "Hey, I just thought of something," she said.

"What?"

"You could invite Tom in here, or we could all go to Tom's room!" Courtney said excitedly. "It would make it so much easier, you know, two guys, two girls. I wouldn't have to try and figure out what to say to him every minute! It's perfect!"

"Gee, Tom's pretty sick—" I began.

"You visit him, so he must be able to have visitors!" she told me. "Oh, please say yes, Star. Please, please, please. I can't talk to him by myself, I really can't!"

What could I do? I said yes.

"Oh, thank you!" Courtney cried. "You're terrific! There's no one else in the whole world like you!"

"Yes, well, I'll, um, just go clear things with Tom," I said, backing out of the room, my IV rolling with me.

How had I gotten myself into this?

I walked down the hall until I stood in front of 2-B. All I had to do was go into that room and get the guy in there to be my boyfriend. The guy I had never even met. The guy that no one had seen. A complete stranger who was maybe so sick, he couldn't come out of his room.

Okay. I could do that.

I took a deep breath and knocked on the door.

6

"Come in," called a young male voice from the other side of the door.

I pushed the door open.

Omigosh, omigosh, omigosh, Tom Levine was gorgeous. He had on faded, ripped jeans and a light blue polo shirt that matched his eyes. He stopped reading *Tennis* magazine and looked at me expectantly.

"Hi," I said, giving him my best rock-video-babe-type smile.

"Hi," he said back.

So far, so good.

"I thought I'd stop in and introduce myself," I said, "since you never come out of your room."

He frowned.

"I mean, it's fine if you don't come out of

your room," I assured him quickly. "I love to be alone myself."

"So why are you here, then?" he asked me.

"Well, I don't love to be alone all the time," I explained. "My name is Star," I added.

"Tom," he said.

Silence. I was just standing there. I didn't know what to do.

"So, Tom," I said finally, "what are you in for?"

"What are you in for?" he asked me.

"Cystic fibrosis," I told him. "It's this lung thing. No big deal."

"It's not a lung thing, actually. It's a disease of the exocrine glands, affecting the pancreas, respiratory system, and sweat glands," Tom said. "A genetic flaw makes your body produce a thick mucus, which clogs up your lungs."

I stared at him in shock. "You've got it too?" I asked.

"Nope," he said.

"Then how—"

"My sister," he said. Something in his face seemed to close when he said that.

So we had something in common. I wheeled my IV pole over to a chair and sat down uninvited. "You still didn't say why you're here," I pointed out.

He looked away from me, out the window. "Because I can't sleep," he mumbled.

"You what?"

"I can't sleep," he repeated evenly.

That didn't make any sense to me. Everyone slept.

"You can't sleep?" I repeated.

"I can't sleep and you can't hear," he said with disgust.

"No need to get so touchy," I said. "I just never heard of anyone who couldn't sleep."

"Well, now you have."

"So, is that why you don't come out of your room," I pressed, "because you're always in here trying to sleep?"

"Something like that," he murmured.

"Can't you just try to sleep at home?" I asked him.

"Listen, no offense, but you ask too many questions," he told me.

"Maybe you just don't give enough answers," I shot back.

"Hey, I didn't invite you in here!" he exclaimed.

"Yes, you did!" I corrected him. "I knocked on the door, and you said, 'Come in.'"

He scowled at me. I scowled back. So what if he was incredibly, impossibly gorgeous. He was a jerk.

It was a stare-down. I refused to blink.

"You have a hair sticking out of your left nostril," I finally said. A muscle twitched next to his mouth. The next thing I knew he let out a snort of laughter, and then so did I. Soon we were both laughing hysterically.

"You're a very strange girl," he said as his laughter subsided.

"Thanks," I said. I have always considered "strange" a compliment. The next thing I knew, I started to cough. Maybe it was laughing so hard that did it. I started coughing and I couldn't stop. I hate that. I know I must look so ugly. Now I'd never be able to convince him to pretend to be my boyfriend.

He got off his bed and gently rubbed my back as the cough finally subsided.

"Better?" he asked quietly.

I nodded. Sometimes it's hard to have the energy to talk after a really big coughing fit.

"Maybe you'd better go lie down," he said gently.

"No, no, I'm okay now," I assured him breathlessly. I took a big swallow of air and let it out without coughing. "See?" I said, smiling brightly.

He laughed. "I see. You have a great smile."

"Thanks!" I said, smiling my great smile

even greater. Obviously I had misjudged him. He wasn't such a jerk, after all.

I shook my curls out of my face in what I hoped was a provocative manner. I kept smiling my great smile. "So, Tom," I said, "the thing is, I have a favor to ask you,"

"Yeah?" he asked.

I held my breath. "Well, could you, I mean would you . . . would you pretend to be my boyfriend for about an hour this evening?" I asked in a rush.

"Would I what?" he exclaimed.

I jumped out of my chair. "Forget it! Forget I said anything! It was a stupid idea," I said. "It was a joke! Yeah, that's what it was, I was only joking!" I backed my way toward the door as I babbled on like an idiot, my stupid IV pole rolling along beside me.

"You want me to pretend to be your boyfriend?" he asked me.

"Did I say that?" I asked, backing farther toward the door.

"That's what I heard," he said. "Why would you want me to do that?"

"Oh, just this guy is coming over to see my roommate, and I might have said my boyfriend was in this room, something like that," I said, backing away from him all the while. "And my roommate thought it would be more comfortable for her and this guy to hang out with me and my boyfriend," I explained. "But, look, just forget the whole thing, it was a stupid idea."

"I'll do it," Tom said.

"Oof." I backed my tailbone right into the doorknob. "So, I'm leaving, I'm gone, nice meeting you and everything," I said, rubbing my tailbone and fumbling at the doorknob.

"Didn't you hear me?" Tom asked. "I said I'll do it."

"But why?" I asked.

"Because you're cute," he said.

"I am?" I asked. "I mean, thanks."

"You're welcome," Tom said. "So how long have we been together?"

"A few weeks, I guess," I said quietly. He had said he'd do it, and he had said I was cute. Now all of a sudden I felt shy. "Do you actually have a girlfriend?" I asked him. "I'm just curious," I added hastily.

"Not at the moment," he said.

"Star, are you in there?" came Sally's whiny voice from the hall.

"Yep," I called back.

Sally opened the door and walked right over to Tom's bed. I noticed she had put on some mascara and blush and she reeked of perfume.

"Hi, I'm Sally," she said, grinning at Tom.

Her overbite looked very pronounced and cute to me all of a sudden.

"Tom," he said. Tom looked at me. "Is this your roommate?" he asked.

"Oh, no, I'm not Star's roommate," Sally said. "I'm rooming with an absolute child." She rolled her eyes. She looked back at Tom. "I hope Star wasn't disturbing you."

"Nope," Tom said.

"So, tell me all about yourself," Sally chirped at him.

"We're leaving, Sally," I said.

"But I just got here!" she protested. "Why do I always get left out of everything?"

"I'll be back later," I told Tom. "If you're sure it's okay—"

"It's okay," he assured me. "See ya."

"Why are you going back later?" Sally whispered at me in the hall.

"None of your business," I told her, heading for my room.

"Oh, that's the thanks I get for doing your spying for you," she fumed. "I won't forget this, Star," she said, flouncing off.

But I was too elated to be upset about Sally. Tom Levine liked my smile! He said I was cute! He said he'd pretend to be my boyfriend! Who knew where we could go from there?

7

"How do I look?" Courtney asked me nervously.

It was around seven-thirty that evening. My aunt Amy had come by with my mom, and with a terrific selection of gourmet food in hand. Being a girl of my word, I invited Sally to join us for dinner. Courtney was nervous and distracted, since she had no idea what time Jeff would show up. It seemed to take forever to get everyone out of our room so that we could get ready for our double date.

That's what I decided it was—a double date. I had never been on a single date. I had never been on any kind of a date, for that matter. I figured if a guy as cute as Tom Levine agrees to pretend to be your boyfriend, and he tells you you're cute, those are date criteria.

I scrutinized Courtney's white cotton pants,

pink T-shirt, and pink-and-white paisley vest. When we took out her braid, her normally straight blond hair rippled down her back in beautiful waves. She had just added a pink ribbon to tie it back, and she stood there, awaiting my opinion.

"Cuter than Winona Ryder," I told her. She had told me that Winona Ryder was her all-time favorite actress.

"Thanks," she said, her face lighting up with pleasure. "If only I didn't have this stupid IV in my arm." She sighed, eyeing the offending needle and the line that ran to the plastic bag of antibiotics.

"Make it work for you," I told her. "Remember, you are a brave and noble heroine."

"Right." Courtney nodded. "I am a brave and noble heroine." She cocked her head to one side and stared at me.

"What?" I asked her. I looked down at myself. I had on blue jeans, my cowboy boots, and a denim shirt.

"You need . . . something," she mused.

"What?" I asked her. "I love what I'm wearing."

"I know just the thing!" she said, snapping her fingers. "My turquoise chain belt. It'll be perfect." Courtney rummaged around in her suitcase until she came up with this fabulous belt of silver chain links with a turquoise stone on the belt buckle. I looped it through my jeans.

"Sexy!" she pronounced. "It goes with that sort of wild, curly-haired look you have," she said. "Oh, and one more thing!" she cried, taking something from a small box. She handed me a beautiful pair of silver-and-turquoise drop earrings. "Good thing your ears are pierced."

I dragged my IV to the bathroom to look at myself in the mirror. The earrings danced through my copper-colored curls and brought out the blue in my blue-green eyes.

"Wow," I said.

"They look terrific on you," Courtney said happily. "I got them at the coolest little shop on Sumner Street, over by the college. We'll have to go there together when we get out of here. They've got great stuff."

"Cool," I agreed casually.

"We can go to the mall too," Courtney continued eagerly. "There's a big sale at Lizbett's Junior Shop next week. I saw this incredibly cute bathing suit in there—it's hot pink and orange. I don't know if it covers enough in the back, though," she added, making a face. "You know how gross that is. Anyway, you'll tell me if I look like a cow in it, won't you?"

"Absolutely," I promised. "There's nothing grosser than a girl who's trying too hard."

"Yeah, that's totally beat," Courtney agreed. She looked me over admiringly. "I want some cowboy boots too." She smiled. "We're going to have so much fun!"

Maybe it could really happen, I told myself. It wasn't impossible. Courtney didn't know how sick I was. I'd just have to go on a day when I was feeling really good and plan it all very carefully. I refused to think about how I could faint or not be able to breath or even, hideous thought, cough up blood right there in the mall. I just refused to believe anything awful would happen, if only Courtney meant it, and she would stay my friend when she got out of Hope House.

The thing is, I had never had a friend to go shopping with. I either went with Claudia or with Aunt Amy. I'd see girls shopping together at the Somerset Mall, giggling and running around, flirting with guys, eating at the food court. It seemed to me like they were in a candy store, and I just had my face pressed against the window, watching, always watching.

"So, what's wrong with Tom again?" Courtney asked, sitting down on her bed.

"It's this very rare sleeping sickness," I said gravely. "He doesn't like to talk about it."

"How did he get it?" Courtney asked.

"Mountain climbing in Peru with his dad," I said. "But don't ask him about it," I added hastily, "he's very sensitive."

"I understand," Courtney said solemnly. She twirled some hair around her finger. "I wish Jeff would hurry up and get here," she said. "I'm so nervous!"

"We could always sing 'Kum Ba Yah,'" I suggested.

The two of us broke into a lusty chorus of "Kum Ba Yah" and the next thing I knew, there stood The Torturer.

"Good evening, it's time," she said to me ominously.

Evening thumps. I had somehow managed to block it from my mind. What if The Torturer was in the middle of it and Jeff showed up. Now, that would be totally humiliating. And even if I lucked out and Jeff didn't show up until it was over, I'd be all sweaty and disgusting looking. No. I absolutely refused.

"Gee, sorry, I should have called to cancel," I told Ms. Tortunesky blithely. "I'm not doing thumps tonight."

"Of course you are," she said, looming over me.

"No, I'm not," I told her.

"I have no time for your nonsense," she barked at me. "Now, assume the position."

"No," I said evenly, even though on the inside I was scared to death. "And you can't make me."

The Torturer glared at me with her ugly, beady little eyes. Courtney stared at me. I could tell she was amazed at my nerve.

"I'll see you tomorrow morning," I told Ms. Tortunesky dismissively.

"Stella Johnella Grubner—" Ms. Tortunesky boomed at me in a threatening voice.

"Star. My name is Star!" I boomed right back at her. "And I'm not doing it tonight! You don't control me! I control me!"

The Torturer's entire self was vibrating with indignation. I wouldn't budge. Finally she turned on her heel and marched out of the room, making sure the door slammed behind her.

Courtney raced over to me and hugged me as well as she could without upsetting her IV. "You were wonderful! You were fantastic!" she cried.

"I was, wasn't I?" I said. I was grinning so hard, it hurt. I had never felt so good in my entire life. I had stood up to The Torturer, and I had won.

There was a knock on the door. Courtney and I called out, "Come on in!" at the same time. In walked Jeff Lowell carrying a bouquet of daisies.

I checked him out as he handed the flowers to a blushing Courtney. He was about five six, with wavy blond hair that was longish in the front, and short in the back. He wore jeans, a white cotton shirt with the sleeves rolled up, and sneakers. He was very, very cute.

"Hi, Jeff," Courtney said in a shy voice. She looked at the flowers. "I'll find some water," she said. Then she realized that sounded stupid. "I mean, I know where there's water," she added hastily, "of course I know that. I meant I didn't know where to put the water, is what I meant," she finished lamely. She blushed an even deeper red and wheeled around, her IV squeaking after her. "Oh, um . . ." she stammered, unable to figure out where the daisies should go.

"I'll do it," I offered, taking the flowers from her. "I'm Star, Courtney's roommate," I added, as I headed into the bathroom to get a glass of water to stick the flowers in.

"Jeff," Jeff said, taking a chair between our two beds.

"Oh, have a seat," Courtney said. "Well, I

guess you already did," she added. "So," she said, sitting on the edge of her bed.

"So, I heard you were kinda sick," Jeff said.

"Just a little," Courtney assured him. "Don't mind this thing," she added, holding up her arm with the needle sticking into it.

"Okay," he said.

I arranged the flowers on the nightstand and sat down on my bed.

"So," Courtney said again, "um . . . how's school?"

"Okay," Jeff said.

"Oh," Courtney said. She threw me a desperate look. Clearly she needed rescuing and she needed it fast.

"Hey, I've got a great idea," I said, jumping up from my bed. "My boyfriend is just down the hall. Why don't we go down to his room?"

"Gee, what a great idea!" Courtney cried, jumping up. "Isn't that a great idea, Jeff?"

"Sure," Jeff said.

We walked down the hall to Tom's room. Now it was my turn to be nervous. What if he had changed his mind? Even worse, what if he'd forgotten his promise completely?

I knocked and entered his room. "Hi, Tom," I said casually. I introduced everyone to each other.

"Hey, I recognize you," Jeff said. "You play tennis for Culver City High, don't you?"

"Yeah," Tom agreed. "You a player?"

"My older brother played you a few weeks ago—Kevin Lowell, from South?" Jeff asked eagerly. "I saw that match. Man, you were awesome. You beat him in straight sets, and my brother is the best guy on the junior varsity team. That put you into the All-State semifinals!"

"I guess," Tom said, looking uncomfortable.

"Hey, that was really something," Jeff said, nodding his head. "So how were the semis?"

Tom shrugged. For some reason he didn't seem to be into talking about tennis. He looked over at me. "So, how's my girlfriend today?" he asked me, changing the subject completely.

He remembered! Thank you, God!

"Oh, just fabulous," I said with a huge grin.

"Yeah, you're looking hot," he told me. "But then you always do."

"Have you and Star been together a long time?" Courtney asked Tom.

Tom said yes and I said no at exactly the same moment.

"I mean, that depends on what you call a long time," I added quickly.

"Right," Tom said. "The time has gone by so fast that a long time seems like a short time."

"I heard about your younger brother," Courtney said knowingly.

"My younger bro—?" Tom began.

"Yes, you know," I interrupted him. "Your brother. Ken. The one who introduced us that fateful day," I coached him.

"Ah, yes," he agreed, "that fateful day."

"Is he still speaking to you after what happened?" Courtney wanted to know.

This time I said yes and Tom said no at exactly the same moment.

"What he means is Ken doesn't talk about that fateful day, but he still talks," I explained. "Right, Tom?"

"Right," Tom agreed. "I mean, we live in the same house and everything, so he sort of has to."

"Wait until I tell Kevin I met you," Jeff said. He clearly wasn't interested in talking about my big romance. "He told me you were the best player he's ever played."

"It's only a game," Tom said. "It's not important."

"Are you kidding?" Jeff protested. "Kevin says—"

But we never got to find out what Kevin said, because there was a quick knock and then Sally and Alison entered the room. Alison had her guitar in her hand.

"Hi, kids!" Sally called cheerfully. She sat down next to Tom and smiled at him.

"Why, Sally, what a surprise," I said with a big fake grin on my face. "What are you doing here?"

"Oh, I overheard you guys saying there was a party in here tonight," Sally chirped. "Hi, Tom," she added. "Remember me?"

Alison sat on the other bed and started strumming "Kum Ba Yah." "Everybody know this one?" she asked cheerfully. "I'll go over the words. It starts out 'Kum ba yah, my Lord, kum ba yah . . .'"

"What does that mean?" Tom asked.

"Star put you up to this, right?" Alison asked.

"Put me up to what?" Tom asked.

I laughed. "I always ask her exactly the same question!"

"Well, it's a good question!" Tom said. "Why should I sing something when I don't know what it means?"

"That's very romantic." Courtney sighed. "You two think exactly alike! I think it's so cute when couples do that."

"What are you talking about?" Sally demanded. "They're not a couple! They just met!"

"We did not!" I said hotly. "He's my boyfriend!"

"Oh, Star, you are such a big fat liar," Sally hissed.

"Maybe we should try a different song," Alison suggested.

"Star is not a liar!" Courtney said, coming to my defense.

"She is so!" Sally cried. "Star doesn't have a boyfriend!"

"I do too!" I insisted, wishing Sally would just curl up and die.

"Tom's brother introduced them or something," Jeff offered.

"Oh, sure." Sally snorted. "Star asked me to spy on him just this morning, so she could find out about him, isn't that the truth?" she asked, staring me in the face.

"Let's not quarrel, Sally," Alison said. "Let's sing about happy things!"

Sally ignored this advice. Her eyes narrowed as she stared me down. "Why don't you just tell everyone the truth?" Sally taunted me.

"Please tell Sally the truth so she'll shut up," Courtney begged.

Everyone stared at me.

"I—I . . ." I stammered.

Tom got up from the bed and pulled me out of my chair. Then he put his arms around me, and right there in front of everybody, he gave me a kiss.

I actually heard Sally's intake of breath.

"Well, I guess that shows you," Courtney said smugly to Sally.

Sally's lower lip trembled. "Everyone is against me!" she cried, and ran out the door.

As for me, I wasn't paying a lot of attention to Sally. I was too busy recording the moment, being as it was just about the most perfect moment of my life. I wanted to remember every tiny little detail about my very first kiss.

I know we stayed in the room a little longer. I think Alison gave up trying to get us to sing and eventually wandered off looking for perkier patients. Finally Jeff said his dad was waiting downstairs, and he left too.

"Bye," Courtney said as she and I headed to the door of Tom's room. "It was great meeting you."

"Yeah, bye," I said. I looked at the floor. I couldn't seem to look at his face. Tom stopped me and kissed me on the cheek.

"Bye," he said softly.

"He's the coolest guy I ever met in my life," Courtney said as we wheeled our IVs down the hall. "You are so, so, so lucky."

"Jeff is nice too," I told her.

"He seemed so young next to Tom," Courtney said with a sigh.

We got ready for bed. I was still in a daze. I

lay in bed with my eyes closed, replaying every moment of that kiss in my mind. He got up. He put his arms around me. He kissed me. I held my hand up to my mouth and pretended it was his mouth. I kissed my hand. Somehow it didn't feel the same.

"Night, Star," Courtney called to me from her bed. "I had the greatest time tonight."

"Me too," I said. I felt a light cough come up in my throat, but I willed it back. What an evening. I had stood up to The Torturer. I had been kissed for the very first time.

It seemed to me that kiss was above and beyond the call of duty. Maybe it was just wishful thinking, but he really didn't have to kiss me like that to prove he was my boyfriend. Which had to mean that he really, actually, honest-to-goodness liked me.

That need-to-cough feeling welled up again, and this time I couldn't stop it. I coughed gently. Then I coughed some more. I sat up, that usually helped. This time it didn't. I coughed some more. It sounded funny to me, low and gravelly. It kept coming in little waves.

"Star, are you okay?" Courtney called from across the room.

"Sure," I said casually. "Sorry to keep you awake," I managed to add. It was hard to talk. I felt like I couldn't get enough air. *I can con-*

trol this, I told myself. *I refuse to give in to this.*
But my stomach wasn't listening. Suddenly I
felt sick to my stomach and no amount of will-
power could stop the feeling. I coughed some
more. It sounded wet. I gasped for air.

Courtney heard me and she snapped on the
nightstand light. "Star?" she asked anxiously.

*Please don't let me be sick, please don't let me
be sick,* I chanted to myself in my head. But
myself wasn't listening.

"Courtney, I think I'm going to—"

But before I could finish telling her, I started
to throw up. It seemed to happen in slow motion. It kept coming and coming, I couldn't
stop it. It was blood coming out of my mouth,
dark red and black, covering me and the bedspread and the floor. It looked like all the blood
inside of me was coming out. And I couldn't
stop it.

"Oh, my gosh." Courtney gasped. She ran
into the hall, screaming for the nurse.

And I sat there, gasping for breath, covered
with blood, waiting to see if I would die.

8

I was floating, floating on my back in a beautiful pool of warm, aqua-blue water. The sun was shining on my face. Everything felt peaceful, everything felt fine. And then, dimly, I heard the voices.

"The lung infection must have eroded a major artery, which is why she hemorrhaged," a deep male voice said. "It's called hemoptysis."

"But this was so much more than she ever bled before," another voice said anxiously. I recognized that one. It belonged to Claudia. Why did she sound so upset? I didn't want to listen to her voice. I wanted to keep floating.

"Yes, well, you may as well get used to it," the first voice said.

"What he means is that the bleeding isn't so unusual," a soft female voice said smoothly. I recognized that voice too. It was Dr. Ambrose.

"When will she wake up?" Claudia asked.

"Hard to say," the first voice said. "We gave her a pretty strong tranquilizer."

"To stop the coughing," Dr. Ambrose added.

"Yes, it's standard in these cases," the male voice said.

"How soon will Dr. Pembroke be in?" Claudia asked. I could tell from the tone of her voice that she didn't like that guy, whoever he was.

"He's on his way," the voice said. "I'll be back later."

"Why does Dr. Pembroke have that man covering for him?" I heard Claudia ask Dr. Ambrose.

"Dr. Ferrar is really a good doctor," Dr. Ambrose said. "He's just . . . he doesn't know how to talk to people."

"Emily," my mom said, "if the guy can't talk to people, he is not a good doctor."

"Yes, well . . ." Dr. Ambrose said. Doctors never say anything bad about each other. It's like they're all in some big secret club.

"I don't want him touching Star again, ever," Claudia said. "I need a cigarette."

"I have to go check on another patient," Dr. Ambrose said. "I'll be back soon—or just have me paged if she wakes up."

"She won't," said the voice I now knew belonged to someone named Dr. Ferrar. He must have come back into the room and overheard Dr. Ambrose. "She'll be out for hours. I just stopped back in to say you can have me paged if you need me," he said. "Dr. Pembroke should be here shortly."

"Idiot-moron-cretin," Claudia said under her breath. This is Claudia's favorite expression for people she cannot stand. I smiled.

"Star, did you just smile?" Claudia asked me, jumping up from her chair. "You did, didn't you?"

I kept my eyes closed and shook my head no.

"You did too," she said.

I opened my eyes. Everything was starting to hurt. I would have preferred to go back to floating, but Claudia was eager to talk.

"How do you feel, honey? You really, really scared me," she said.

"I'm okay," I croaked. Even saying that much took a tremendous effort.

"Of course you're okay," Claudia said. "Nothing keeps my baby down, right?"

"Right," I agreed. I looked over at Courtney's bed. It was empty. "Where's Courtney?" I whispered.

"I don't know," she said. "Do you remember what happened?"

It all came rushing back to me. The coughing. That terrible feeling in my chest and my stomach. And the blood, blood everywhere. I especially remembered the look of disgust and horror on Courtney's face as she ran from the room.

"How long was I sleeping?" I asked.

"A long time," Claudia said. "It's very late."

I noticed I was wearing a hospital gown, the hideous kind that ties in the back. All the blood had been cleaned up. I must have slept through the whole thing.

Dr. Pembroke hurried into the room. "Well, Star, how are you feeling?" he asked me.

"What took you so long?" my mother demanded. "You should have been here two hours ago!"

"I was two hours away from Somerset, as I'm sure my service told you," Dr. Pembroke said. "Dr. Ferrar was here covering."

"Yeah, well, Dr. Ferrar is obnoxious, and he doesn't know Star," Claudia said.

Dr. Pembroke ignored Claudia and took my hand. "Had a bit of a scare, eh, Star?" he asked me.

"I'm fine," I whispered.

"It must have been scary, though," Dr. Pembroke said.

"Don't tell her to be scared if she's not, for goodness' sake!" my mother interjected.

Dr. Pembroke ignored her. "Do you feel like coughing anymore?" he asked me gently.

I shook my head no.

"Good," Dr. Pembroke said. "The tranquilizer has calmed down your system, so that should help. I think you'll start feeling much, much better."

"Is this because I didn't do thumps?" I croaked at Dr. Pembroke.

He looked confused.

"I skipped thumps," I confessed tearfully. "Ms. Tortunesky came and I refused."

"Star, you can't refuse to do your therapy," Dr. Pembroke said gently.

"This is my fault," I whispered.

"It might have happened anyway," Dr. Pembroke said. "Don't blame yourself, okay?"

I nodded yes, but in my heart I knew it was all my fault.

Ms. McG. came in with her usual bright smile. She laid a cool hand on my forehead. I was so glad to see her.

"Star, dear heart, glad to see you're awake," she said in her beautiful brogue. "I'm going to give you a shot of vitamin K now, it'll help your blot clot more quickly, okay?"

I nodded yes.

"Just a quick stick, dear heart," she said, carefully turning me slightly to my side.

"There," she said. "All done. No more needles." She stroked my hair a moment, then left the room.

"Star, your mom and I are going down the hall for a little while, then we'll be back," Dr. Pembroke said. "Okay?"

I knew they were going to talk about me. Part of me wanted to yell that since I was the one who was sick, the least they could do was not talk about it behind my back. But another part of me didn't want to know, and so I didn't say anything.

I lay there, staring at the ceiling. I knew I had had a very close call, closer than ever before. It was just too scary to think about, too impossible.

"Star?" It was Courtney, standing over my bed. Her eyes looked huge, staring down at me.

"Hi," I said quietly.

"Are you okay?" she asked.

"Sure," I said, trying for my usual breezy style. "So, what did I miss while the lights were out?"

She gave me a strange look. "Why are you making jokes?"

"Why not?" I shrugged.

"Why not?" she echoed. "That is a stupid thing to say! You scared me to death!"

"Oh, puh-leeze," I said, rolling my eyes. "What's a little blood between friends?"

"Friends?" she repeated angrily. "We're not friends."

I knew it. I knew it would happen if she found out how sick I was. Everything was completely ruined, and it was my fault, all because I skipped one stupid session of thumps.

"Okay, we're not friends." I shrugged. "No biggie."

"Time for another tranquilizer, dear heart," Ms. McG. said, coming back into the room. "You need to rest."

I sat up and took the pill, completely ignoring Courtney. I didn't need her. I didn't need anybody. That's what I kept saying to myself as I drifted back to sleep.

No one was in the room when I woke up, and it was light outside. My head was pounding. I heard noises in the hall. Sally was yelling to someone that she had saved a pancake from breakfast to use as a Frisbee. That was a stupid thing to say. Ms. Brady's strawberry pancakes are fabulous. Sally was just showing off as usual.

And if Sally was yelling about breakfast, that meant I had slept through the night. Everything that had happened came back to me, but

I remembered it in a fog. I knew it was from the tranquilizers they'd given me. I remembered the part about fighting with Courtney, and I could hear her voice in my head telling me that we weren't friends. That seemed like the worst part of all. I guess I should have known it was all just a stupid fantasy, anyway.

"You're awake," Courtney said, coming in the door.

She looked different. For just a moment I couldn't figure out why. Then I realized she was no longer hooked up to an IV.

"You must be better, they took your IV out," I said.

"I guess," she said. "My arm's sore where the needle was."

"So I guess you're getting out soon," I said.

Courtney shrugged. "I have to have more tests today. But Dr. Steve said my EKG looked good. I have a lot more energy."

"Good," I said. She was just staring at me. I felt like a bug under a microscope. So what if she didn't want to be my friend, that didn't mean she could act any old way she wanted. I mean, I was not begging for friends, thank you very much.

"Listen, Star—" she began.

Why should I give her the satisfaction of telling me all over again how we weren't really friends? Or even worse, why should I listen to her lie and say she'd come and visit me when she got out? I had heard those lies before.

"Listen, Courtney," I interrupted her. "I'm going to be pretty busy working on this new play I'm thinking about writing. A lot of important people are interested in it. So I don't think I'm going to have time to go shopping with you or anything. No offense."

She looked at me like I was crazy. "Why are you talking about shopping? Why are you acting like such an idiot?"

"You're the idiot!" I screamed.

"I'm not the one who almost died!" she screamed back.

"Look, the freak show is over, okay?" I said viciously. "So just leave me alone."

I turned my head away from her, but I could hear her standing there, just breathing. "Why didn't you tell me?" she asked in a low voice.

"Tell you what?"

"How sick you are," she said.

"It's not exactly any of your business," I told her. "Besides, I'm not that sick."

"You're not?" Courtney asked. "Then why have you lived practically all your life in Hope House? Sally told me the truth, you know."

"Sally should be cut into little pieces and added to the Thursday-night meat loaf," I said.

Courtney ignored my humor. "Why don't you go to school?" she demanded.

"I told you why," I said, "because I'm an actress—"

"That's not why," Courtney said. "It's because of your cystic fibrosis. Why don't you just admit it?" she cried.

"All it means is that I cough sometimes—"

Courtney looked angry enough to punch me. She grabbed a folded-up piece of paper from the back pocket of her pants, unfolded it, and read what was written there out loud.

" 'Cystic fibrosis is a disease of the exocrine glands. They keep producing mucus and clog up the lungs, creating an ideal breeding ground for viral and bacterial pneumonias. Eventually antibiotics can no longer fight the pneumonias. This disease is fatal. Cause of death is either severe bleeding from the lungs, which results in the patient choking to death, or eventual heart failure.' "

There was silence in the room.

"So, did you want me to grade you on your paper?" I asked her sarcastically. "I give it a B-minus. Sort of simplistic, doesn't cover any new ground, fairly well written," I said.

"Why didn't you just tell me the truth?"

"I don't owe you anything," I snapped.

Courtney gulped. "I guess not," she managed. "But it's just that I—I thought you really cared about me. I was so scared coming here, and you made everything okay. You even made it fun sometimes, and then I wasn't scared anymore." She stared down at her sheet of paper. "I thought we were going to be best friends. I thought I was so lucky, because I had never met anyone like you before in my entire life. But you didn't even care about me enough to tell me the truth."

"But you hate sick kids!" I protested.

"I never said that!" she cried.

"You did too!" I said. "You were so glad your roommate wasn't sick. You said the kids who had cancer looked so gross because they lost their hair. . . ."

Courtney bit her lip. "I didn't mean it," she whispered.

"Yes, you did," I said. "What was I supposed to say? 'Guess what, Courtney, I'm one of them!' "

"I didn't know. . . . I—I didn't understand. . . ." she stammered.

"Well, most kids don't," I snapped. "Which is exactly why I don't tell anyone."

She pushed her hair behind her ear and scuffed her shoe against the floor. "I guess you don't want to be friends with me after all, then," she said.

"You're the one who told me we weren't friends," I pointed out.

"Because I thought you just lied to me for no good reason," she said, "but I was wrong." She wandered over to her bed and sat down. "I must have made you feel terrible."

"Look, it's no big deal," I told her.

"So I guess you wouldn't want to hang out with me when I get out of here," she said, "after how stupid I was."

My heart was beating faster, and it wasn't because I felt sick. Could she possibly want to be my friend after all this? I decided on the cautious approach. "That depends on how stupid you are," I said. "Are we talking Sally-type stupid here, or are we talking there's-hope-type stupid?"

"There's hope . . . I hope," she said with a grin.

"Okay, then." I swallowed. "I guess I could hang out with you."

"We'll have a blast!" Courtney said, bouncing on her bed. "We'll go to the mall, we'll go to the movies. It just has to be on a day you're feeling okay, right?"

"Right," I agreed.

"So then . . . no problem!" she said, imitating me.

"You might just forget all about me when you

leave here, you know," I told her. "It's happened before."

"I could never forget about you," Courtney said fervently. "There's no one else like you in the whole world."

Her eyes were shining at me. And something wonderful happened. I actually believed her. We really were going to be friends.

9

"Oh, Julie, you should see how cute Star's boyfriend is. Really, he is totally awesome," Courtney said.

It was a week later, and I was feeling much, much stronger. I wasn't coughing very much, except at night. Courtney was feeling a lot better too. Dr. Steve had told her she'd probably be released soon, so she was in a great mood. Three of Courtney's friends had come over, and all five of us were eating a pizza, compliments of Aunt Amy. Julie was sprawled on Courtney's bed, Stacey was in a chair, and Beth was sitting cross-legged on my bed with me. It was so terrific. Courtney was including me in everything. And because she was including me, her friends were too.

"He's so mature," Courtney said with a sigh.

"You guys should see him. He's fifteen," she added significantly.

"He came to visit you?" Julie asked, her mouth full of pizza.

I shot Courtney a look. I didn't want them to know that Tom was in Hope House. "Right," I said. "In fact he was here at the same time as Jeff." Well, at least that much was true.

"It was so cool, the four of us hung out together," Courtney said.

"Jeff really, really likes you," Julie told her friend.

"How do you know?" Courtney demanded.

"Well, he was talking about you in school," Stacey told her.

"He was?" Courtney asked. "Tell me everything he said, word for word."

"Yeah, surely you taped the conversation for her!" I said.

Everyone laughed.

"You guys, cut it out!" Courtney said, but she had a huge grin on her face.

"He was talking to a bunch of us at lunch yesterday," Stacey said. "And he said how you were so brave about being sick, and how he really admired your attitude."

"Omigosh, it worked!" Courtney said with a laugh. "It was all Star's idea!"

"Gets 'em every time," I said knowingly.

"We better get going," Julie said. "My mother the motor-mouth is down in the lobby. She's probably told everyone who's passed by the story of my life by now."

"I wish we could stay," Beth said. "It's so much fun here."

"Yeah, you lucked out, Courtney," Stacey said. "We got twenty pages of geometry homework."

"So, when are you guys getting out of here, anyway?" Julie asked. "We should have a party, or something."

Courtney's eyes lit up. "Hey, I've got a great idea! I should give a party after the school dance next week—you know how early it'll end —and Star can come!"

"Your mom will never let you give a boy-girl party," Julie said. "She probably says prayers every night that you'll become allergic to the entire guy portion of the population!"

All Courtney's friends giggled.

"True," Courtney agreed, "but these are what you call extenuating circumstances, after I was so gravely ill and all," she added dramatically, throwing one hand to her forehead.

Huh. Decently done, I thought to myself. Maybe I had actually taught her a thing or two.

"Seriously," Courtney continued. "My dad

will convince my mom. I know he will! And it'll be so cool if you come, Star."

"Could you, Star?" Julie asked. "Oh, it would be fabulous!"

"I'd have to check my datebook," I said coolly.

Courtney threw a pillow at me. "Come on, say you'll come."

"You talked me into it," I said.

"I'll call you later and we'll plan it," Julie promised.

The three girls hugged both of us and left.

"You'll be okay, won't you, Star?" Courtney asked anxiously. "For the party, I mean?"

"Yeah, they'll spring me for a party, unless I'm in really bad shape," I said.

"Great!" Courtney cried. "And no one even has to know you're in Hope House, unless you want them to. Oh, you should invite Tom!"

"Oh, gee, I, uh, gee, I don't know . . ." I stammered.

"Of course you should!" Courtney said. "He and Jeff get along great. Let's go ask him now!"

Uh-oh. It was one thing to pretend that Tom was my boyfriend in Hope House, and quite another to expect him to continue the charade out there in the real world. Even I could only be so audacious. I mean, I had never been to any kind of a boy-girl party, much less one with a date.

Another thing was that Tom hadn't made any effort to see me or talk to me since we were in his room. I didn't know if he knew how sick I'd been or not. But I figured if he really liked me, he would have knocked on my door by now. After all, what with his not sleeping he had to have a lot of free time on his hands.

Courtney sat there on the edge of her bed, looking so hopeful and enthusiastic, that I made a decision. If we were really, truly friends now, then I owed it to her to tell her the truth. I just prayed she would understand why I had pretended that Tom was my boyfriend.

"Courtney, there's something I should tell you about Tom," I said. "See, the thing is, I lied."

"You lied?" she asked me, her eyes wide.

I nodded. "He isn't really my boyfriend."

"But I saw him kiss you!" she protested.

"I guess he's a good actor," I said with a shrug. Then I explained how I had gotten carried away with my own story, telling her that my boyfriend was in 2-B. I told her everything, how I'd gone to his room and he'd agreed to go along with me and pretend to be my boyfriend. "So, that's it," I finished. "Do you hate me?"

"Are you kidding?" Courtney cried. "That's,

like, the greatest story I ever heard in my life! You got this incredibly cool older guy to pretend to be your boyfriend, and he even kissed you! He must have just decided he really liked you! I would never have had the nerve in a bazillion years!"

I laughed. "Yeah, I guess it was pretty nervy. But I don't think he really likes me. He was just being nice."

"I think you're wrong," Courtney said. "When you got so sick, I ran down to his room. I figured he would want to know. He was really, really concerned. He's the one who gave me all that stuff I read to you about cystic fibrosis. He told me he wrote a paper about it once."

"I was wondering how you got all that information so fast," I said. Then something clicked in my head. Suddenly it all made sense. Tom. And me. And his little sister who had cystic fibrosis.

"I have to go talk to Tom," I told Courtney, getting off my bed and wheeling my IV toward the door.

"Is something wrong?" Courtney asked.

"I'll tell you later," I promised, and headed for Tom's room.

"Come on in," he called when I knocked on his door.

"You're a jerk," I told him as I entered the room.

"Hi, very nice to see you too. Glad to see you're feeling better," Tom said with a wry look on his face.

"Yeah, like you care," I snorted, my hands on my hips. The needle from the IV pulled on my skin. I didn't care. "Look," I said, "I don't need any more merciful gestures from you, okay?"

"What are you talking about?" he asked me.

"Don't pretend you don't know," I said. "You are such a liar. 'You have a great smile. You're really cute,'" I said, mimicking him perfectly. "You must think I'm really pathetic!" I yelled.

"I don't think that at all," he said quietly.

"No? Where's your sister, the one who has cystic fibrosis?" I challenged him.

"She doesn't have anything to do with this—" Tom began.

"Oh, yes, she does," I interrupted him. "Where is she?"

He was silent for a moment. "She's dead," he said finally. "She died three months ago."

"And that's why you wrote that paper on cystic fibrosis, because of her, right?" I asked him.

"I was trying to understand," he said.

"So you think I'm going to die, just like your

sister, and that's why you pretended to be my boyfriend, why you pretended to like me," I fumed. "It was all because you felt sorry for me!"

"You've got it wrong, Star—"

"Liar!" I screamed. "Well, I've got news for you. I'm not going to die! And I wouldn't have you for my boyfriend if you were the last guy on earth!"

He stared at me a moment. "Look, you're right. When you told me you had CF, it reminded me of my sister—"

"I knew it," I snarled.

"—And I guess I did agree because of that—but only at first. Then I just liked you," he said.

"Yeah, I bet," I snorted.

"I did," he insisted. "I mean, I do. You really are cute. And funny. And you have a great smile."

"Oh, I guess that's why you've been hanging around my room ever since the last time I saw you, because you like me so much," I said sarcastically.

Tom ran his hand through his hair and looked out the window. "Sit down a minute," he said.

"I don't want to sit down," I said sullenly.

"Please," he added.

I sighed dramatically and sat down. "Well?"

He sat on his bed. "My little sister, Jessie, was the cutest kid," he began softly. "I was really crazy about her. Only, she was born with this horrible disease. I never really believed she'd die—it just didn't seem possible. But she did. She was eleven years old. It was right before I was supposed to play in the tennis regional semifinals. You know how unimportant that seemed, in the scheme of things? Everyone was saying how great I was, and how brave I was, and it made me sick. I haven't played tennis since. And I haven't slept much either."

"You mean this sleeping thing is in your head, because of your sister?" I asked him.

"That's what the brilliant doctors say," he said sarcastically. "But I don't think my head is sick. I think it's my heart."

"So am I supposed to feel sorry for you?" I demanded.

"Am I supposed to feel sorry for you?" he shot back.

"No, you moron!" I cried. "That's the whole point."

He stared at me. "You're a real pain, Star, but I'm done feeling sorry for you, okay? I like you because . . . I just do."

I tried to decide if I believed him. "Why haven't you come to my room, then?" I asked him.

"I was scared," he admitted. "Because I like you. And I was afraid to like you too much. . . ."

"In case the same thing happened to me that happened to your sister," I finished for him. I got up from the chair. "Well, you can do whatever you want, but like I said, I'm not dying." I brushed some hair out of my eyes. "You know, if you take the attitude that something bad might happen if you care about someone, then you'll never care about anyone."

Tom walked over to me. "So would anything bad happen if I kissed you again?"

I shrugged, trying my best to look cool. "I guess that's a chance you'd have to take."

So he kissed me.

10

"Okay, I've got twenty names on the list," Courtney said, chewing on the eraser end of her pencil. "You think that's too many?"

It was Friday evening a week later, and I had just finished my evening thumps. As usual I was exhausted and sweaty. It was wonderful not to have to hide how I felt from Courtney anymore.

She had asked her parents if she could have a party after the school dance, and wonder of wonders, they said yes right away. Even her mother didn't give her a hard time. She was so happy Courtney was coming home that she would have agreed to anything.

"Twenty is a good size," I decided. "Do we have the same number of guys and girls?"

"Yeah, now that Tom is coming," she said happily. I had invited Tom to the party two days earlier, and he had actually said yes. He told me he'd slept the night before without a tranquilizer. He would be going home soon.

Courtney was due to be released the next day. But now that we were planning this party together, I really believed that we were going to stay friends. It was like I said to Tom—you can't worry that something bad will happen if you care about someone. Well, maybe I had done that myself in the past. But I was changing.

"Okay, let's figure out the refreshments," Courtney said. "They'll only have the world's crummiest punch and stale cookies at the school dance, so everyone will be hungry and thirsty by the time they get to my house."

"Yeah, but let's not serve messy food, because all the girls will be afraid to eat," I said.

"Good point," she said. "Burgers?"

"Fried chicken bits?" I ventured.

"Yeah, your aunt Amy's bits!" Courtney cried. "If my parents will spring for it, that is."

"Hey, I have pull with the chef," I said, laughing. "I know we can get a great price. In fact, if I ask Aunt Amy I'm sure she'd do all the refreshments."

"Can you imagine twenty Tall, Dark, and Chocolates?" Courtney giggled.

"With mountains of double-chocolate Oreo-cookie ice cream," I added. "Mmmm, it sounds so good, who cares if it's messy?"

Sally stuck her head in the door without so much as a tiny knock. "Hello," she said. "What are you two doing?" This was a little strange, since Sally and I had been sort of avoiding each other for the past two weeks.

"Nothing much," Courtney said, slipping the party list under her pillow. No way were we inviting Sally.

Sally wandered over to the window, then she came back and stood by my bed. "I just wanted to say . . . I know it's been a while and everything, but I'm sorry about what I said about Tom," Sally said in a rush. "I didn't know he was really your boyfriend. I thought you were just lying. But he explained to me later that he really was, and when you asked me to find out about the guy in 2-B, you had no idea it was him."

"He said that?" I asked in shock.

"Uh-huh," Sally said.

"Well, it would have been mean, anyway," Courtney told her.

"Oh, yeah?" Sally said. "Well, well . . ." Sally could not think of a comeback. I decided to let her off the hook, being as she was IQ-free.

"It's okay, Sally. Thanks for telling me," I said.

"Hey, you guys want to go to the rec room and watch TV?" Sally asked hopefully.

"No, thanks," Courtney said. "Maybe later."

Sally looked so sad as she scuffed her way out the door. And it was funny—instead of feeling irritated by her like I usually did, I felt sorry for her. She was so lonely. She was as lonely as I had been before I met Courtney. Maybe she showed it differently, and maybe she wasn't too smart, but we had more in common than I wanted to admit.

"Wait a minute, Sally," I called to her. "We're planning a party at Courtney's house next Saturday. Do you want to come?"

Courtney looked at me like I was crazy, but fortunately Sally didn't notice. She was too busy staring at me, her face lit up like a Christmas tree.

"Are you serious? Really?" Sally asked eagerly.

"Really," I assured her. "It'll be fun."

Sally looked shyly over at Courtney. "Is it okay with you too?" she asked.

"Sure," said Courtney, without missing a beat.

Sally grinned gratefully at Courtney, then at me. She looked pretty cute, overbite and all. And she didn't even look all that stupid, once she felt like we might actually like her a little. Imagine that.

"That was a very nice thing you just did," Courtney said to me when Sally had left the room. "You're a good person."

"Yeah, well, don't let it get around," I told Courtney with a grin. "My rep will be shot."

Courtney threw a pillow at me. "You know, it was so cool of Tom to tell Sally he really had been your boyfriend all along, don't you think?"

"Yeah, I do," I said with a small smile.

"So, look, let's get to the really crucial stuff," Courtney said. "We have to figure out what we're going to wear to this party. I wonder if we can plan a shopping trip to the mall," she mused.

"If I go after afternoon thumps and before evening," I said. "And if I'm having a good day and not coughing too much. Did Dr. Steve tell you you could do anything you want now?" I asked Courtney.

"Pretty much. I have to keep taking oral antibiotics at home. I'm not supposed to exert myself too much. He wants to keep monitoring my heart, so I have to come in for tests next week. Anyway, I don't have that icky tired feeling anymore."

"Howdy, kiddos!" my mom called as she

dashed into our room. She dumped a load of books and papers on the nightstand. "Compliments of Liza-Jayne," my mom said. "Dr. Pembroke says you're well enough to start with your tutor again tomorrow."

"Gee, great news," I said sarcastically.

"Hi, Claudia," Courtney said. "Whoa, fabulous outfit," she added, eyeing Claudia's beige suede fringed vest and matching miniskirt.

"Thanks," Claudia said, sliding into a chair. "I got it shipped to me from New York."

I knew that. It was her good-luck New York outfit. And she wore it only for very, very special occasions.

"What happened?" I demanded. "I know something happened. It's Broadway, right?"

"No," Claudia said.

"Off-Broadway?" I asked. "So, that's still fabulous!"

"Sorry, baby, not that big," Claudia said. "I got the lead in the new play the Somerset Community Theater is doing. You are looking at Fanny Brice in *Funny Girl*!"

"Oh, this is terrific!" Courtney said, jumping off her bed to hug my mother. "We'll come see it together, won't we, Star?"

"Sure," I said. "Absolutely."

I tried to look happy for my mother, but I knew how disappointed she was. Another lead in another community theater production. Well, how could she go to Broadway with me around, anyway? I mean, sure, they have good doctors in New York. But when I'm home Claudia spends so much time with me doing thumps, she couldn't do a real show. I never said this out loud, of course, and neither did she. It was another one of those things we never talked about.

"So how are you feeling, baby?" she asked me.

"Much better," I said. "Almost no cough all day."

"That's great!" she said. "I knew you'd beat this! I'm going to ask Dr. Pembroke if we can break you out of this joint, maybe before Courtney's party."

"Would you?" I asked her hopefully.

"You got it," she told me. "Hey, want to go for a walk?" Claudia asked me, jumping out of her chair. "I'm all antsy tonight."

"Sure," I said easily, even though I actually felt very tired. I turned to Courtney. "Want to come?"

"No, I've got to do that geometry homework Julie brought by for me," Courtney said, making a face. "Honestly, I don't see what geometry has to do with anything," she grumbled. "I mean, not knowing what an isosceles triangle is has never ruined anybody's life.''

"Right," I agreed. "It's not like it's anything really important, like, say, having good fashion sense.''

Courtney laughed. "If I got graded on that, I'd be on the honor·roll!" she said. "Anyway, if I finish up quick I'll come find you, if that's okay.''

"No problem," I assured her. "And I'll be sure to tell your mommy what a good girl you were, doing your homework first and everything," I added wickedly.

"Get out of here!" she yelled good-naturedly.

I laughed and waved to her as Claudia and I headed out the door.

"You two have really gotten to be good friends in the last few weeks," Claudia said, helping me wheel my IV as we headed down to the rec room. They always served punch or milk and cookies down there around nine o'clock. On the rare occasion that Ms. Brady baked homemade oatmeal cookies, they disappeared immediately.

"Yeah, isn't she great?" I asked Claudia. "You know, it seems like I've known her forever. I can't imagine my life anymore without her as my best friend, you know? She and I are going to have a blast when she gets out. I can't wait."

"Good, babe," my mom said. I wasn't sure whether she believed me—you know, thinking I was getting my hopes up too much—maybe she was just distracted about something else.

"She really is going to be my friend, you know. Not just while we're in Hope House."

"That's great," Claudia said.

Oh, so that's all she was going to say. Maybe I was supposed to pretend that I actually had friends my own age, so that Courtney's friendship wouldn't be such a big deal. Maybe I wasn't supposed to notice how I always hung out around my mother's friends, or Aunt Amy's friends. So this was evidently just another thing we weren't supposed to talk about. Okay. I could deal.

"So, you psyched about this part?" I asked my mom, changing the subject completely.

"Sure," she said, not very convincingly.

"Well, what happened with that big phone call from New York you were expecting?" I asked.

Claudia shrugged. "That's show biz," she said lightly. I could see anxiety etched across her face. "Boy, do I ever wish I still smoked."

"So what are you upset about?" I asked.

"I'm not upset," she said as we turned the

corner to the rec room. I could hear the TV blaring, and Alison's voice calling to people to come to Sally's room for a sing-along.

I peeked into the rec room. "Store-bought chocolate-chip cookies," I said wrinkling my nose.

"Let's skip it and go down to the living room," my mom suggested.

We got on the small elevator that was reserved for kids with IVs or kids in wheelchairs. Claudia was silent all the way down. Claudia is never silent.

"I wish you'd tell me what's bothering you," I said when we got into the living room.

Rachel Harris was sitting on the other side of the room with her parents and Andrea Shepherd. Rachel was fidgeting around on the couch and her mother was going on and on about something in a voice too low for me to hear. Andrea kept nodding in that understanding way she has. I noticed that Rachel seemed to look right through her mother, as if she could make her disappear by an act of will. It was very creepy.

We chose a couch near the fireplace, far on the other side of the large room. Claudia looked at Rachel out of the corner of her eye.

"That poor kid," Claudia said in a low voice.

"Imagine starving yourself practically to death."

"I can't imagine it," I said. "I love to eat too much." I looked over at Rachel, who was staring at her mother. She had such a look of hate on her face. "Wow, she really hates her mom," I said.

"I'm so glad we're friends," Claudia said. She opened her purse and rummaged around for hard candy. "That's how I think of you, you know," Claudia said. "You're my best friend."

I smiled, but I didn't really feel like smiling. Something about Claudia's saying that always made me uncomfortable.

"Really," Claudia continued. "You've always been unique that way. Sometimes I think you're more grown up than I am!" She found the candy and popped one in her mouth.

"So then why won't you tell me what's bothering you?" I asked her.

Claudia laughed. "You amaze me. You can read me like a book. I guess I'm just feeling—I don't know—old."

"Because you didn't get the phone call from New York?" I asked.

"It's silly," Claudia said. "I should be glad to get the lead in community theater musicals. But you know, once I had all these dreams. . . ."

"It could still happen," I insisted. "You can't just give up on your dreams!"

"No, but sometimes you have to be realistic and modify them," she said wryly. "I'm not kidding myself anymore. There are girls arriving in New York every day who are younger than me, and prettier than me, and probably more talented than me. I'm not going to get any phone call."

I wanted to say it out loud so badly: "It's because of me. I ruined your life. I ruined your dreams." And I was even starting to get up the nerve to say it, when Dr. Steve came into the living room.

"Star!" he said, his face breaking into a grin as he walked toward us. "Hi, Claudia," he added.

Dr. Steve took the chair next to me. Please note that he could have sat down next to Claudia, but he didn't.

"I've been swamped for a few days, I haven't seen too much of you," Dr. Steve said. "How are you feeling?"

"Marvelous, fabulous, terrific," I said breezily.

Dr. Steve laughed. "You are one of a kind. Courtney says the two of you have become great buddies."

"She did?" I asked with pleasure.

"Yeah, I hear you're planning this blowout party together," Dr. Steve said.

I nodded happily. "It's going to be awesome," I told him. "Twenty kids are invited, and I have a date with—"

"Code red, code red," came over the intercom system. "Dr. Rhodes, second floor, stat."

Dr. Steve got up immediately and ran out of the room and up the stairs. I could feel all the color draining from my face as I stared after him. Code red meant there was an emergency. One of Dr. Steve's patients was in big, big trouble.

"I wonder why they never say the room number when they call a code," my mom said faintly. Her face looked as drained of color as mine did. No matter how many times you hear a code red called, you never get used to it.

"I figure it's because they don't want to scare all the other kids by letting them know who might be about to kick the bucket," I said.

I stared at the ceiling, as if I could see upstairs to the poor, scared kid up there who was a code red. I noticed Rachel across the room was doing exactly the same thing. Andrea reached for her hand. It was as if we were all holding our breath. I sat there wishing whoever it was would be okay. There was always a chance. After all, the last code red called at

Hope House had been for me, and I was around to talk about it.

Rachel looked over at me. "It's my roommate, I just know it. She had open heart surgery," she said. "Oh, no . . ."

So that's who the code was for. I hadn't even known that Rachel had a roommate, I guess because the roommate was so sick, she'd been confined to her bed. I swiftly sent up a prayer for that poor, scared kid.

"I wasn't even nice to her," Rachel continued. "I thought she was dweeby."

I didn't know what to say. Andrea just held on more tightly to Rachel's hand.

"Code red, code red," the voice repeated over the intercom.

"I can't stand it," Rachel said, jumping up. "I have to go see if it's Hillary."

"You know they won't let you in the room," Andrea said. "And I'm sure Dr. Steve is doing everything he can."

"I have to go up there," Rachel insisted. "I was mean to her. I made fun of her." Rachel was practically in tears now, heading for the elevator as fast as her IV would allow.

For some reason I followed her, as if maybe I could watch over her and make sure she was okay. I don't know why I did that. I didn't even particularly like Rachel Harris. But it was as if some bond tied us together, something that my mother and her parents and even Andrea couldn't really understand.

The elevator doors opened onto the second-floor hall, and we walked as quickly as we could toward Rachel's room. I expected to see a huge commotion, but there wasn't one. There was just a pale young girl asleep in her bed.

Rachel and I looked at each other. It wasn't Hillary. And there wasn't any commotion in her wing. As if by unspoken agreement we headed for the other side of the house. We turned the corner to the hall that led down to my room. And there at the end of the hall were nurses running in and out, loud voices, frantic activity. There was the code red.

It was my room. It was Courtney.

11

"Let me go!" I screamed. "What are they doing in my room?"

I was standing right outside my door. Tom was holding my arms, and I was struggling against him as hard as I could.

"Something happened to Courtney," Tom said.

"That's crazy! That's nuts!" I screamed. "Courtney is fine! She's going home tomorrow!"

A small group of kids was huddled outside the door. They knew enough to stay out of the way, and were pressed against the wall. Sally reached out and touched my hand, but I shook her off. Little Alex Fury had his hands over his eyes, as if he could make everything go away.

"Come on, kids, go back to your rooms," Dr. Graham was urging everyone.

Inside the room I could hear Dr. Steve counting. "One, two, three, four . . . defibrillate her again!" he yelled. Then he counted some more. "Give me a reading!"

"Blood pressure zero, pulse zero," Ms. McG. said. I heard the high faraway sound of a buzzer going off. "We've lost her," Ms. McG. said in a desperate voice.

"No!" I screamed, fighting with Tom all over again. "There's nothing wrong with her!" I insisted.

The kids in the hall started to wander back to their rooms. Dr. Graham put his arm around Alex and led him away. No one was crying. Everyone was silent. Death wasn't such a stranger to the kids in Hope House.

Dr. Steve came out of my room. He looked like he was about to cry.

"What did you do?" I demanded. "I want to see her!"

"I'm so sorry, Star," Dr. Steve said. "Courtney's heart was damaged by her illness. Her chorda tendinea ruptured. There was nothing we could have done." He was shaking his head and I could see the tears in his eyes.

"But that can't be true!" I shouted. I could feel the hot tears cascading down my cheeks. "Please, make it not be true!"

"I'm so sorry," Dr. Steve said again.

I finally broke away from Tom and dashed into the room. Courtney was in her bed. At least that's who they said it was. A white sheet was pulled over her head.

My mother was behind me. "Come on, baby, come out of there," she said, gently leading me away from Courtney.

"No, she can't breathe!" I yelled. "Take the sheet off of her face!"

My mother led me out into the hall. "It's okay, baby, it's going to be okay," she crooned to me.

I stood there crying. I cried so hard, my whole body shook and I couldn't catch my breath. I wanted to be tough. I really did. But I just couldn't this time.

"It's okay," Claudia said again.

I pulled away from her. "No, it's not! Nothing is okay! Don't you understand? She was my friend! She was my very first friend!"

"It's okay, baby," Claudia said, reaching for me. "I'll be your friend."

I stared at her for a moment. Then it was if something snapped. "No!" I screamed savagely. "I don't want you to be my friend! I want you to be my mother!"

There were tears in Claudia's eyes. "I am, Star, I am," she assured me.

"No!" I screamed. "You never wanted that.

You're Claudia, and I ruined your life. I want Courtney! I want my friend!" I turned, blinded by my tears, and ran into Tom. He put his arms around me.

From behind me I heard a noise, and I turned. Two nurses were wheeling Courtney somewhere.

"Don't touch her!" I yelled at them. "Don't hurt her!"

"We won't hurt her, Star," Ms. McG. promised me, her face wet with tears.

Tom stroked my hair and held me tight. But it didn't matter. Nothing would ever be okay again. The world was too lonely, too scary. I didn't know where to turn.

And then I felt Claudia's hand on my shoulder, slowly turning me toward her. I looked at her face. And the worst pain in the world looked back at me.

Normally I would have done anything, said anything, to take that pain off of Claudia's face. But I just couldn't do it this time. I stared at her.

"I'm so sorry," Claudia whispered.

"No—"

"Yes," she said. "It's okay not to be strong now, honey," Claudia said. "It's okay to be scared."

"No—" I insisted. I couldn't let go. I couldn't

look all the sickness and death and loss in the face. It was just too scary. I had tried to pretend for so long that everything would be okay. If I let that go, the whole world would go crazy.

"Yes," she said firmly. "It's okay." She held out her arms to me.

I took a step toward her.

"I'm your mommy, Star," she said gently. "I always will be. I'll always take care of you. I'll never leave you."

I ran into her arms.

She held me while I cried. "I'm so afraid. I'm afraid I'll die." I sobbed. "I don't want to die. I don't want them to cover me up with a sheet like they did to Courtney."

She held me in her arms, and we cried and cried.

The pretending was over.

EPILOGUE

Courtney's funeral was two weeks ago. There were hundreds of people there. I sat in the back with Tom and the kids from Hope House. Even the staff from Hope House didn't sit in the same row we did. Courtney's friends and family sat up in the front, apart from us. And I guess they really were apart from us in a certain way, and they always would be. Those of us kids who lived in Hope House lived in a country that they would probably never know.

I've been out of Hope House for ten days now. Tom has come over twice. I really like him. But what's even more amazing than that is that Courtney's friends, Julie and Stacey and Beth, have been coming over too. I went to the mall one day with Julie. And Stacey just invited me to her birthday party next week. Even if I do live in another country, sometimes it's fun to pretend that I live in theirs.

And sometimes I wonder . . . what would have happened if Courtney had lived, and we'd had a chance to do all the things together we wanted to do? But I can't change what happened any more than I can change that I have cystic fibrosis. It's just the way it is.

I tried to make a list of all the great things about Courtney, but it looked stupid on paper. I mean, what was the point? How could I ever really explain what she'd done for me, just by being who she was? Courtney had liked me for myself. All she wanted from me was to be my friend. I didn't have to hide anymore, or pretend that I wasn't really sick, or that I wasn't scared of dying. She accepted me completely, just as I am. And something about her accepting me made me start to accept me too. It's just about the greatest gift anyone ever gave me.

And I believe that she knows, and she's smiling down on me right now, telling me I should enjoy every moment of my time on this planet, however long it is.

Thanks, Courtney. No problem.

AUTHOR'S BIOGRAPHY

CHERIE BENNETT is the author of many novels for young adults and middle readers, including the best-selling series Sunset Island. She is also an award-winning playwright. She is married to Jeff Gottesfeld, a theatrical producer and an attorney. They have two fat cats, Trinity and Julius. After living in New York City for many years, Cherie and Jeff recently moved to Nashville, Tennessee.